Ellen Kuzwayo grew up in the country, but has lived most of her life in the city. She has been 'disgruntled school-teacher', social worker, mother, wife, and in her sixties returned to study at the University of the Witwatersrand for a higher qualification in social work where, in 1987, she was awarded an Honorary Doctorate in law.

She was detained without trial under the so-called 'Terrorism' Act in 1977, when she was 63 – an experience which helped her to feel for and with the young generation of anti-apartheid campaigners who were imprisoned with her.

Today she is active in the community life of Soweto. She is president of the Black Consumer Union of South Africa, and chairman of the Maggie Magaba Trust. She was chosen Woman of the Year in 1979 by the Johannesburg newspaper *The Star*, and was nominated again in 1984. She has helped to make two films directed by Betty Wolpert, 'Awake from Mourning' and 'Tsiamelo: A Place of Goodness', both of which have had international distribution.

Her autobiography, *Call Me Woman*, was published by The Women's Press in 1985, and won the prestigious CNA Prize in South Africa – the first time the prize had been won by a black writer.

GW00707435

Happy reading.

both these women are
exceptional Yet their formative
Years are Continents apart...

Ellen Kuzwayo

Sit Down and Listen

The Women's Press

First published by The Women's Press Ltd 1990
A member of the Namara Group
34 Great Sutton Street, London EC1V 0DX

British Library Cataloguing in Publication Data
Kuzwayo, Ellen, *1914–*
   Sit down and listen.
   I. Title
   823 [F]

ISBN 0–7043–4230–8

Printed and bound by BPCC Hazell Books Ltd,
Member of BPCC Ltd, Aylesbury, Bucks, England

I dedicate this book to my six grandchildren – Ipeleng (*be joyous*) Moloto; Bakgatla (clan name) Moloto; Merafe (*nations*) Moloto; Refilwe (*gift*) Moloto; Peteni (*named after his grandfather*) Kuzwayo; Boitumelo (*joy*) Kuzwayo – and to all the children of my nation, with the hope that they will grow to appreciate and value their heritage and the beautiful country that God has given them.

It is their duty to commit themselves to an education, and to the national struggle, so they can earn liberation and that of their people.

Contents

	Introduction	ix
PART ONE	The Meaning of Cowardice	
	Ask the ostriches	3
	In retrospect	15
PART TWO	Waiting at the Altar	
	Life – a riddle	25
	A double dealer	35
PART THREE	What is a Family?	
	Education – no substitute for culture	47
	One of many	63
	The reward of waiting	75
	The strongest link in a chain is its weakest point	83
PART FOUR	How Much Does a Roof Cost?	
	Choosing a hat for a husband	99
	Granny Basadi	105
PART FIVE	A Person is a Person Because of Another Person	
	Lasting impressions	113
	Life for the black youngsters of that era	125

Introduction

Things happen, people tell stories about them. Then – life passes quickly – the events and stories are faintly remembered or totally forgotten.

But in the black communities of South Africa perhaps we remember our stories for a little longer than other people do. After all, for so many years now, we have owned our stories while owning so little else.

In my lifetime I have seen so many changes, heard so many stories that I wanted to trap some of them on paper before they vanished for ever. There were stories from my youth in the country – stories of the ghosts and unearthly creatures with which some children with imagination like to frighten themselves. There were stories of women with more than one husband and men with more than one wife. And, of course, there were stories, stretching back to the earliest years of this century, of the black people of South Africa, uprooted from their land of wealth and plenty, taking the long, hard road that led finally to the squalor of the townships depicted by abject poverty and human depredation.

These were some of the stories I wanted to tell. And I wanted to tell them in the kind of atmosphere that I remember so well from my youth on my grandparents' farm. Let me tell you a little about this. We all looked forward to the evening story-telling session, adults and young people alike. We would meet together, family and neighbours, at a chosen hearth and, relaxing in front of the fire, we would listen to someone telling us a story – it could just as easily be a legend about our ancestors or a tale about something that had happened the week before. Legends and folk-tales were very popular forms of entertainment in those days.

These presentations were punctuated by moments of great excitement. Having coaxed her listeners into attention, the narrator would fall silent for a moment and adjust her position slightly, moving her stool forward or back. At this point you could hear all the people in the room breathing together – one long, deep breath. All eyes would be glued on the storyteller, willing her to carry on with her tale, desperate to know what happened next. And the air would be full of sighs and sounds of 'Hmmm', 'Ahhh', and 'Eeeh', depending on the mood of the narrative. Meanwhile, the storyteller reached for her shawl, moved her stool, enjoying the full knowledge that her audience was in the palm of her hand.

This was a good way to bring the day to a close, all of us together despite the differences between us. These sessions provided opportunities of great learning for the youth of that era living in a country which for so long has been broken up into discriminatory racial compartments, where land was forcibly removed from ownership of blacks, by whites who were sold to greed and materialism at any cost, to a point of grabbing such land for themselves without any shame or remorse.

I hope that this book will serve as a reminder to those of us who share these story-telling traditions as well as a window through which those who have been brought up to look inwards only can peep and learn a little about their neighbours.

Part One

The Meaning of Cowardice

Do you know what a coward is? I am not so sure. I think that not one of us knows when we will be cowardly and when we will be brave. And I think, too, that intimidation, humiliation and injustice can grind people down to the point where despair blocks the rise of courage. When one man sticks out his chest and raises a rhinoceros whip and another runs away, perhaps you can tell me who the brave man is?

The two stories which follow describe situations in which particular men are judged by some to be cowards. The first story, 'Ask the ostriches', concerns events that happened over eighty years ago – but even then black people in South Africa were largely prevented from controlling their own destinies. As you read the story, you may want to think hard about the fact that the brave man holds a position of responsibility in a self-governing and settled community, while the coward has always been at the beck and call of his white master.

The second story, 'In retrospect', takes place in the early 1950s when the Nationalist Government was introducing new, brutal and systematic methods of controlling the lives of black people. Reverberations echo down from the past and reach forward to the present day. In the traditional culture of black people, respect for parents and older people has pride of place. But how can young people feel this respect in their hearts if they see their parents disregarded, despised and persecuted? Many parents have fought against the injustices forced on them; and some have been victorious. But many others have been ground down by the difficulties and cruelties facing them. And their children have been left bemused, grieved and disappointed, looking for a new source of inspiration and courage.

The women in both these stories have much to suffer. They are caught between the traditional ways and the new, clinging to the old expectations that their man will protect them but fated to realise that, in the end, such protection can bring no lasting safety.

Ask the ostriches

At the turn of the century, large settlements of black people would be found on land owned by white farmers. Some of these people would have lived there all their lives; others would be temporary dwellers in the settlements. The people were labourers on the large fields cultivated on those farms, working with different crops according to the season.

No one knew how long they would be allowed to stay in a settlement. They could remain there only as long as their employer needed their services and approved their stay. And it was common practice – particularly in the harshly oppressive Orange Free State – for white farmers to dismiss their farm labourers at short notice or with no notice at all. For this reason, groups of black people were often seen on the roads, roaming the countryside in search of work or somewhere to live. They could be families, friends or just fellow-travellers – anybody could be in the position of suddenly having no home or no means of support.

Mokote's family of three – father, mother and son of about nine months – was one such family. They were just at the start of a desperate journey to seek out new work.

Long before sunrise on a winter day, they had started their journey from *bass* (master) Jan Bottor's farm. The farmer had given them their *trek pass* (removal document) late the previous afternoon, with firm orders to be off his land that day. The weather was very cold and the family's neighbours had taken pity on them. They offered to keep the family for the night – on condition that they were on their way very early the next day before the *baas* was up. This kind offer could have cost the neighbours their home and employment.

So, on this bitterly cold morning, Mokete's family walked from the farm in single file. The husband carried a stick in one hand, while with the other he supported the few blankets that they owned, slung over his shoulder. The wife, Mookho, with her baby strapped to her back, carried on her head the cud-box packed with their household utensils. These included two small three-legged pots, a bucket for carrying water, a few clay pots, enamel dishes and mugs and a small collection of spoons and knives made from cheap metal. In a container with a handle, she also carried some *sethathabola* (sour porridge). This was used both as food and drink.

Why had Jan Bottor dismissed Mokete – a man who had served his master since early youth? The reason was that Mokete had absented himself twice from work that week because of a chronic chest complaint, a condition which had been reported many times before to the farmer. Jan Bottor had never offered any advice or help to Mokete and, after he had dismissed him, he met with harsh rejection his employee's pleas for mercy and forgiveness.

So Mokete left the farm that had been his home for ten years, bitter, angry, sick and helpless.

During the long, tedious journey that followed, the family happened to meet a traditional medicine man. On hearing of Mokete's illness, he offered him some powdered medication to take with water. After taking the medicine for three or four days, Mokete felt a good deal better, and had gained new strength and courage for the travel that lay ahead.

Once or twice on their journey, the family was fortunate enough to be offered food and overnight shelter by labourers on the farms they passed through. But there was no work available on these farms. Most of the other nights they spent in the open *veld*, taking shelter from the cold in old, ruined houses or under a tree where they could light a fire to keep out the harsh winter cold. It was a miracle that their little baby survived.

After one particular night out in the open, they woke to a day of unexpected mildness. They decided to remain under the shade of the tree that had been their shelter the night before. Here they prepared their morning meal of mealie-pap and well-cooked rabbit: Mokete had gone hunting the day before. As they sat chatting, almost forgetting their sorrowful plight in the warm rays of the sun, Mookho suddenly raised her head as if she was frightened. 'Do you hear a strange noise?' she asked her husband. 'A noise like the hooves of some angry animal?' Mokete strained his ears to catch the noise, but all in vain. And, hearing nothing, he dismissed his wife's fears and carried on eating. But Mookho could still hear the noise and was ill at ease.

All of a sudden, the noise reached Mokete's ears. Startled, he jumped up and looked in the direction from which it came. In a high voice, he shouted to his wife, 'Mookho, *dimpshe* (ostriches)!' and in the wink of an eye he was ready to run, picking up his stick but leaving all their 'wealth' behind. Mookho paused only to strap the baby on her back and grab hold of the porridge container. They dashed in the same direction, running away from the long-legged birds which lazily, but swiftly, followed their footsteps. Mokete kept waving his stick wildly at the creatures, hoping to frighten them away. Before long, he ran past his wife, with the ostriches still hot on their trail.

Mookho ran for dear life, screaming for help at the top of her voice. Mokete looked back once; but he was too frightened to go back to assist his wife who by this time ran for dear life, from the menacing ostriches.

As Mookho scrambled up a slope, she thought she saw a flock of sheep in the distance. Again she screamed for help, hoping that someone was in charge of the flock. Her husband was now nowhere to be seen. The first ostrich caught up with her as she approached a fence – her last hope of protection. Still screaming and clutching her howling baby to her back, she failed to jump the fence. With clumsy fingers she unstrapped the baby and threw him over the fence; and then turned to struggle with the ostrich that was about to trample on her.

She had resigned herself to the worst when, out of nowhere, a man appeared. In a moment, he lifted the baby and placed him out of reach of the biggest and tallest ostrich. Then he acted swiftly to rescue Mookho from the bird before the rest of the ostriches arrived. He battled furiously with the big creature; while Mookho also kicked and pushed with her hands and feet, giving the ostrich no opportunity to take full hold of her. By some miracle, the man found the strength to drag the woman over the fence to his side while all the time she kicked, screamed and pushed at the ostrich. The infuriated creature ran along the fence in a desperate attempt to reach Mookho; and it was soon joined by the rest of its family. Disillusioned after a while, they moved slowly back to where they came from, stamping all the way.

The hero of the day turned out to be the owner of the flock of sheep that Mookho had seen, or thought she had seen, at the height of her fright. He turned to her, asking, 'Woman, what happened? Where do you come from? Why do you travel alone in this wild land? White farmers here own furious dogs which can tear you apart in a second.' He put so many questions to her that she found it difficult to reply. She was too shocked to speak and was concerned first of all with calming down the baby who was still sobbing and very frightened. The man left her to calm down as he attended to his flock.

On his return, he pursued his questions, wanting to know why this woman moved alone with her baby. Finally, she related her story to the stranger as it had happened. He listened to her without believing what she was saying. He suddenly heard himself say, 'You mean you were with your husband when these birds attacked you? Is he your husband? Is this his son?' The woman confirmed that she had been with her husband, the father of her son. The man sighed deeply and said, 'I find it difficult to believe this.' Mookho answered quickly and with tears, 'But he is my husband and I do not know where we shall find him.'

Her baby was still crying and very fidgety. Turning towards her, the man said gently, 'Woman, sit down and calm your baby. With his father gone, he is your closest relative now. I still cannot understand how a father can leave his family to the vultures of the air. How could he leave a woman carrying his baby in such a plight?' As Mookho cried and moaned at his words, the man comforted her, saying, 'Calm down and stop crying, woman.' He moved away to collect his flock in preparing for turning homewards.

When he came back, he found her breast-feeding the baby. She was sobbing quietly and tears trickled down her cheeks. The man sat down and took out his snuff-box, offering some to Mookho. 'Have some snuff,' he said, 'it might soothe your hurt.' She took some, saying, 'Thank you,' amid tears and sobs.

They sat there, not exchanging a word for some time. Then the man said, 'I am Thulo and, who are you?' She replied with her name. The man continued, 'It is time for me to move my flock home. I cannot leave you here alone. Pick up your baby and let us go.' As she strapped her baby to her back, Mookho wept, saying between sobs, 'Perhaps my husband has taken refuge in your village.' The man nodded his head and said, 'Perhaps. Who knows?'

Reluctantly, Mookho stood up, all the time looking around as if in search of her husband. She walked slowly behind Thulo as he steered his flock in the direction of the village. As they approached the settlement and some of the houses came into view, Mookho suddenly broke down and started to weep from the heart. Her young son soon joined in her sobs.

Finding himself in this predicament, Thulo called to some boys to herd the sheep into the *kraal*, while he rushed home to share with his wife the events of the day. He asked her to go with him to calm the strange woman who seemed unable to control her emotions. Together they did all in their power to comfort Mookho and her son; but with very little success.

By this time, a growing crowd of people from the village was adding to the problem. Some came close to enquire about what they saw; others stood far back, trying to put two and two together. Many different stories were concocted. Some said that Thulo had found himself a new young wife and that they had been living together at some strange village. Now he had brought her home with their new baby. Others told a similar story – but with a slant to explain why the woman was weeping. Yet another version had it that Thulo had fought and killed the woman's husband and that was why she was crying so bitterly.

Puleng, Thulo's wife, listened to all these fabrications as she worked hard with her husband to calm and comfort Mookho. Knowing her husband as she did, Puleng took no notice of any of the stories – although even she was rather taken aback by the tale of the ostriches.

After two or three hours – they seemed like days on end – Puleng managed to persuade Mookho to go to their home for the night. She held out the hope that Mookho's husband might hear of her extraordinary arrival in the village and come to find his family. Once there, all efforts to plead with Mookho to take something to eat failed; and in the end Puleng took Mookho's son from his mother to comfort him and try to feed him.

Thulo was not only a successful farmer but also the right-hand man of the Chief (King) of the Bakwena tribe who lived in that region. He discussed with his wife the wisdom of going immediately to report the incident to the King. Husband and wife agreed that this was the right course to take.

Years after the fateful day, Mookho told a friend of her hopes and fears at that time. This is what she told her. Her greatest hope on that day was the sudden appearance of her husband, coming to the village from nowhere. Her greatest fear was of being hounded by the white farmer who owned the land where Thulo lived. It was with great joy then that she discovered that her hosts' home was in a village owned and administered by the Bakwena tribe under the rule of their King. This revelation sustained Mookho through all her feelings of loss, insecurity, estrangement and loneliness. It enabled her to settle down, accept her fate and start life over again.

Within a year, she became a member of Thulo's family. Her friendliness, honesty, reliability, industriousness and openness of mind won her many friends in the home and community. At the same time, her son, Tefo, became part of the family and grew up with the other youngsters as if he had been born among the Bakwena people. He was the only boy in Thulo's home: Thulo's other children were three daughters. With the passing of time, Thulo became very attached to Tefo; and Tefo was like a brother to the three daughters. Mookho herself felt so much at home that she shared in the chores of the household without hesitation or question. In Mookho, Puleng found a helper, friend and confidante.

In that community, polygamy was not common; but it was not unknown, and it was not frowned on. In those days, a husband who wished to take another wife would first consult his present wife to find out if such an arrangement was acceptable to her. In some cases, the first wife would herself suggest that her husband take a particular woman as his second wife; and many such unions have brought happiness and harmony.

Two years after Mookho joined the family – and two years in which no husband arrived – Puleng told Thulo how much she loved and admired Mookho; and she suggested to him that if he took Mookho as his second wife, the joy and prosperity of their home would be increased even further. This suggestion came as a surprise to Thulo; but he greatly welcomed such a gracious and generous thought from his wife. He played down his excitement and joy in order to avoid any suspicion that his thoughts had already moved in that direction. His response to his wife's offer was: 'Puleng, my wife, before you can make a suggestion like this, you must weigh it up carefully. Besides, Mookho's husband may show up at any minute. What would happen then?'

Puleng made a quick reply. 'Thulo, are you saying that you do not see what I see in Mookho? Her husband! I don't think that he would recognise his wife any more, let alone his son. The boy is not a baby now; he is a very lovable youngster and our daughters' brother. I would not give him away for anything.' Thulo wondered if Puleng had said all these things to Mookho. Without much thought, he responded, 'Never say that to Mookho. She will be cross and believe that we are taking her for granted. She is very fond of her husband.' As if in anger, Puleng retorted sharply, 'He must go and ask the ostriches where his wife is, not us.' Thulo burst out laughing.

After this conversation, Thulo made a firm decision which he never shared with anyone. He decided not to refer to the subject until Puleng raised it again. Whilst waiting for Puleng to reopen the discussion, his love for Mookho devoured him. Soon Mookho began to notice something unusual in his manner and behaviour towards her. She saw too that Thulo was particularly warm and loving towards Tefo, her son. His changed behaviour caused Mookho great concern. But she dared not raise the matter with Puleng for fear of creating a rift between them, close friends as they were.

A month or two later, Puleng remarked to her husband, 'Thulo, you mean that you have never given thought to what I said to you about Mookho?' Her husband replied, 'Puleng, I have. But before I can do anything, I must go and report to the King that, two years on, Mookho's husband still has not turned up. And then I must ask his advice of what the next step should be.'

Puleng turned slowly to look into her husband's eyes. 'Thulo,' she said, 'I admire you for not making a hasty decision. Much as I love and admire Mookho, the last thing I would want is for you to rush into this union without weighing up the whole matter carefully.' At her words, Thulo was seized by a sudden fear that his wife might read him wrongly and think that he was not interested in Mookho. He answered her quickly: 'Puleng, I want to thank you for this generous offer. I must admit that since you broached the subject, I have given it thought and wondered if you meant every word that you said.' When Puleng confirmed that she had spoken from the heart, Thulo decided that he would immediately approach the King about the matter and seek his guidance.

The King gave an unhesitating response to Thulo's case. 'I have long waited for these words from you,' he said. And looking up at Thulo, he continued, 'My candid opinion on the matter is as follows: I have great admiration and respect for you as my right-hand man. First, you rescued Mookho and her son from the wild birds which could have killed them. Then you brought them to your home, despite the insulting rumours running through the village. And since that time, you and your wife have taken the wanderers into your family. Judging by Mookho's involvement in your home and her warm relationship with your wife, I would say that she is a remarkable woman. Such a situation is rare and amazing. If Mookho's husband ever comes here with questions, my reply to him will be, "Go and ask the ostriches where your family is." Thulo, if you let this woman go, you will be throwing away your God-given fortune.'

When Mookho had been accepted as Thulo's second wife for about a year, she found that she was expecting his child. There was great joy in the whole family. One evening, at twilight, Mookho had just finished serving the evening meal and the family was sitting round the glowing fire, chatting. When the calm was disturbed by the persistent barking of the village dogs, Tefo and his friends went to investigate. Finding nothing, they continued with the evening's entertainment. But then the sound of rushing, furious dogs shattered the peace of the village. '*Voetsak, voetsak, voetsak*,' the command used to reprimand dogs, was heard from all sides as a dark figure was seen approaching the homestead. Thulo immediately instructed the boys to ensure that the dogs did the stranger no harm.

From the dark, a voice said, 'Greetings at home.' The head of the family responded, 'Good evening, gentleman.' Appearing ill at ease, the stranger took a seat in an obscure corner. After the usual formalities had been exchanged – 'How do you do?' and so on – a long silence followed. Thulo broke the silence by asking Mookho, 'Mma Tefo, is there no food to offer the stranger?' Reluctantly, Mookho stood up and arranged a simple meal for the guest. When she approached him to offer him the food, their eyes met, and she recognised in this ageing and dilapidated man her first husband. He had given a different name from 'Mokete' when he had introduced himself. Mookho kept her peace and continued to play her part in the calm family evening. But she was disturbed and shaken, deep down. Did Mokete recognise her? she wondered. And, if he did, did he know that this was her home? Was he coming in search of her and her son? All these questions span around in her head.

Mokete was offered shelter in an outside room reserved for tramp-like guests. Next morning, the family woke to find their guest sitting alone in the corner of the verandah. When the head of the family joined him and tried to make conversation with him, the stranger said very little but appeared to be loaded with worry. Every time Mookho offered him a meal, a task assigned to her, Mokete tried to speak to her. Each time, she quickly left him, without saying a word.

On the third day, as Thulo continued to question him about his situation, Mokete became very agitated. In the middle of a disjointed conversation, he blurted out, 'I am looking for my wife and son. I think I have found them.' Startled by this unexpected statement, Thulo turned to his guest, saying, 'Where?' Mokete replied, 'Here, in this home.' 'You are wrong, sir,' Thulo replied.

Feeling very helpless and inadequate, Mokete lost his temper and started to shout and make a scene. As crowds of villagers gathered along the road to watch this strange performance, Mokete shouted out at the top of his voice that Mookho was his wife, Tefo his son and he had come to fetch them back home.

Cool and collected, Thulo addressed Mokete in the following words: 'Before you remove Mookho and Tefo from this home, you will first tell the *kgotla* (court) where you get the power to do so. Not before then will you be allowed to take them away.' Confident of his case, Mokete readily agreed to Thulo's suggestion and expressed his desire to lay the matter before the ruler of the village.

The King and his councillors gathered in the courtyard to listen to Mokete's case and pleas. The court had listened for some time to Mokete's angry and vulgar hectoring when the King interrupted to ask one question: In what circumstances had Mokete last seen his family? Without hesitation, Mokete gave an accurate account of what had happened the day the ostriches attacked himself and his family; of how he had left his wife and son behind while running away from the huge, fierce birds.

The King called a crowd of boys of Tefo's age to stand before him. He ordered Mokete to identify his son in the crowd. Mokete took a long time to decide where to point his finger; and in the end he chose a young boy who bore some resemblance to his son.

At that point, the King ordered Mokete to stand up and face him. 'Sir,' said the King, 'this young man here' – he pointed at Tefo – 'and his mother sitting there' – he pointed at Mookho – 'were rescued from the furious ostriches by that man.' He pointed at Thulo. 'Go and ask the ostriches to give you your family back. And leave my village at once, you coward.'

In retrospect

Looking back, we can all find a new land in the past. At the time, we often take events, big or small, for granted and dismiss them from our minds as if they did not matter. And then suddenly – days, weeks, months or even years afterwards – they come sharply into focus and we see them again with new eyes. In this clear daylight of the mind, we see strange connections between past and present; we see undreamt-of patterns in our lives and the lives of the people close to us.

So it is with something that happened to me over thirty years ago. At the time, I felt sorry for the young people involved and embarrassed for myself because I was placed in an awkward position. Now I see – and feel – much more. I see a link in a chain of cruelty manacled to my people, a chain forged with the aim of destroying us as a people. And I feel grief. And I feel anger. Constantly, I have to check myself from being devoured by bitterness.

It happened in the early 1950s when I was working for the once-renowned Non-European Affairs Department – at that time a wing of the Johannesburg City Council. The responsibilities of the Department included running the recreational section for the young people who lived in the growing complex of Soweto.

I worked with the youth of the community – which was my community too. The young programme for boys and girls, aged from eight to about eighteen, included traditional drama, dance and song, modern music and dance of European origin, clay modelling and other hand work crafts, and weekend outings and sea-side camping during the Christmas school holidays. In those years, this last activity was particularly popular among the youths of the black community, coming as they did from the most deprived section of the country's population.

One of the venues for weekend camping was the Wilgespruit Fellowship Centre. This was one of the first centres in South Africa to promote interchurch and Christian-orientated programmes for adults and young people. Wilgespruit has for many years been under the spotlight of the security and police in the country. About three years ago, helicopters hovered over that centre in search of young people who were in sanctuary there. Some were detained, then harassed and traumatised in detention. Others died in the operation.

It was to this centre that I went one weekend, all those years ago, with a party of forty to fifty boys and girls from Orlando and Pimville – separate townships then, but now part of Soweto.

Following our arrival there on the Friday evening, the boys invited me to join them at their campfire. I remember being taken aback by this request: it was customary to have a large gathering round the campfire on the last rather than the first evening of the weekend. I failed to get an explanation for this change in the proceedings; but I accepted the invitation, since the young people seemed very anxious for me to join them. I was curious, I remember, and also a little nervous.

At the appointed time, we all gathered round the fire. At first, the conversation was casual, even idle; but it was as if everyone but me knew that something of significance was going to happen later. I searched my mind in vain, trying to guess the purpose of the meeting. Gradually, the empty, idle talk petered out. One of the boys – let me call him F.D. – then welcomed me formally into the group and thanked me for accepting their invitation. The formality with which I was introduced brought with it a feeling of gravity and importance. I remember trying to prepare myself mentally for what was clearly gòing to be a serious discussion.

Normally, my dealings with members of the clubs were casual and relaxed. The young people addressed me either as 'Ma K' or as 'Mistress', the customary way of addressing a lady teacher in the black community, and often shortened to 'Mistry'. This was an inheritance from my time as a schoolteacher; and it was a form of address which I quite liked as it carried with it something of the feeling of goodwill between the teacher and her pupils. But I remember feeling happier later on in our discussions when I was addressed in the usual friendly way as 'Ma K'.

For the moment, I kept my peace and listened carefully to what followed. 'Ma K,' continued F.D., 'I have asked you to be here with us this evening with the permission of my friends. I want to share something very personal with you and the group. I hope that you will respond to what I have to say by telling me what you would do and how you would react if you were in my position.' Each sentence F.D. uttered spelt out the seriousness of what he was about to lay before us.

He went on to describe a shattering experience which he had gone through along with his family. I had heard of similar events being endured by other families; and I knew that such events were not uncommon in many urban areas inhabited by black people. But F.D.'s first-hand account brought home to me the deep meaning and pain of the experience. And now, today, thirty years later, his story has new and frightening echoes.

Listening to a story of this kind from one of my club members carried a particularly sharp sting for me – all the more so since F.D. gave his account in a composed, simple and truthful way. I was amazed by the maturity of this young boy as he related an experience so personal, humiliating, insulting and infuriating without bursting into sobs of anger or grief. I was sweating and sighing to the point of weeping as I listened to him. There were moments when, overcome with disgust, horror and shame, I bowed my head until my eyes were nailed to the fire. The other members of the group listened attentively, occasionally moaning or sighing with anger and disgust. Every time I lifted my head, I found that shame prevented me from looking those young people in the eye. Yet, in a mad way, I felt supported by the maturity, respect and consideration I sensed all around me. They sat there quietly, exchanging glances and gestures without uttering a word. In their silence, I felt that I heard them say, 'Yes, Ma K, there it is. Tell us. Where do we go from here?' I was numb.

F.D. started his story by describing his mother and contrasting her with some of the sophisticated women in his community. His mother was quite unlike those of us employed in youth club work, he said, continuing, 'My mother is not educated, and she is not sophisticated in any way.' It became clear that she was a simple, traditional mother who followed the habits and customs handed down to her from earlier days. She would not dream, for example, of wearing a nightdress or morning gown – the kind of clothes which her son had seen other women wear during camping weekends. This quiet woman's life, he told us, had been attacked at the heart – in her home

Two months before, at about two o'clock in the morning, the family was woken from deep sleep by a sharp knock on the door, accompanied by shouts of '*Vula! Vula lomnya-ngo wena* (Open up! Open this door, you . . .)'. At first, in their confusion, the family struggled to think of who could be assaulting them in this way, at that hour. But they soon realised that, like many families in their community, they were being 'visited' by the notorious 'black jacks' from the Municipal Superintendent's office in the township.

The name 'black jacks' is given to all black municipal police employed in black urban areas. The unpleasant name is well-deserved. These are the people who hound out families at ungodly hours; charge them with having broken one law or another; collect one or two members of the family, depending on the nature of the alleged offence; put them into the council vehicle; and move on from house to house, collecting yet more residents who are alleged to have committed offences. Finally, the black jacks deposit their 'load' at the municipal office at about four o'clock in the morning; the people can then do nothing but wait for the arrival of the white superintendents from the city at 8.30 or 9.30. The long, drawn-out business of interrogation then begins. This was the normal routine for any alleged offender – and, in some places, it still is.

F.D. told of the shock suffered by his family at the violent arrival of the black jacks. The moment the policemen gained entry into the house, they opened all the doors, kicking open those that were secured by a lock. They harassed all the inmates of the house, using obscene language to adults, children and toddlers alike; and, after each curse, they yelled out commands like, '*Vuka! Vuka! Sihambe! Sheshisha, sheshisha!* (Wake up! Wake up! Let's go! Hurry! Hurry!)'. He described vividly the turmoil, confusion and terror which resulted from that harassment; the house was like an 'open show', he said. The parents' bedroom door was kicked wide open; while the older children in the opposite room struggled to get themselves dressed, all the while trembling and sobbing.

It was at this point that F.D. experienced his moment of deep horror – a moment which remained seared in his mind, causing him endless torment and fury. What happened was this. While he was hurriedly getting dressed, F.D. looked towards his parents' bedroom – and felt immediately that he was in the heart of a bad dream. He forgot about the other children round him; he forgot that he was in the middle of dressing himself; all he could do was stare fixedly, unwilling to believe his eyes, at the scene before him. 'All passed very quickly,' he said, 'but it happened.

'There stood my poor mother – a woman who for her whole life had loved and respected her children. A woman who had never had any need for nightdresses or gowns. She stood there, terrorised by the black jacks, doing all in her power to cover her loins with a shawl. But her hands were trembling with fear and shock and the shawl kept slipping out of her grasp. She tried again and again to cover her naked body; but all in vain. And there was my father – someone I had loved and respected and always looked to for support and protection – standing there like a reed blown by the wind, trembling from head to foot; watching my dear mother trying hard to cover herself up, pushed around by the cold-hearted, disrespectful municipal police. My mother was in terrible distress; and my father looked on without raising his voice or a finger to protect her from humiliation in front of these insulting black jacks.'

By that point, I was soaked with perspiration and bent over with shame. I was filled with revulsion at the thought that a black son – for those policemen too must have had mothers – could behave like that to a black mother. But there was more to come.

As if from a distance, F.D. turned to me and addressed me directly. I could feel the eyes of the whole group focus on me. Carefully and clearly, he asked me, 'Ellen Kuzwayo, my question to you is – if that was your father, how would you regard him?'

I felt then as if F.D. had dropped a bombshell on me. I must have looked blank, confused and stunned. My body and my mind were suddenly acutely aware of the eyes of the group turned intently towards me. The dead silence round the campfire brought home to me the importance of my response for all those young people. Somehow I knew that they expected me to offer some sort of magical solution to the painful dilemma in which both they and I found ourselves; and indeed many thoughts passed through my mind with the speed of electricity. But it took me a very long time to find any words to share with the young people.

In that deep silence, I formulated one sentence after another, dismissing each one before uttering it as I realised that my words were hollow and full of contradictions. My mind – and my tongue – were blocked by the knowledge that the loyalty of a son to his father was at stake. I did not know F.D.'s father, but from what I had heard from his son, he seemed to be a caring and loving parent, with his family's welfare at heart. I felt a very strong urge to protect his image, to save him from rejection by his children. At the same time, it was undeniable that he had failed to challenge, even in a mild way, the arrogance and insulting behaviour of those municipal police. Deep down, I accepted that F.D.'s father had acted in a cowardly way. But I could not bring myself to say so to the group. Perhaps I was a coward myself. But, not knowing the man, I was hesitant to pronounce judgment on him – and, by so doing, damn him further in his son's eyes and mind.

Eventually, I turned to F.D. and said, 'Perhaps we should not be too hard on your father, by judging him on the basis of this single unfortunate incident. We all react differently to situations. And he was certainly taken unawares, thrown into a state of shock like the rest of your family. All the same, I can understand your concern for your mother. It is real and proper. What I am saying is that this one incident should not be the basis for rejecting and condemning your father.'

As I had feared, F.D. was unconvinced by my words. He remained hurt and angry at his father's unprotective stance as head of the family; and, in particular, at his father's failure to protect the mother of the family. Although they did not say much, his friends clearly shared his feelings. They believed that, like many other black parents, F.D.'s father had failed his family. They saw a general failure by black parents and other adults to take a firm stand against any form of intimidation, humiliation and injustice perpetrated by those in authority or by their representatives.

Part of the true meaning of that experience in the 1950s fell into place for me only in 1976, when the black youth of Soweto took the reins into their own hands. In an explosion of energy and determination, they expressed their frustration, anger and sense of utter helplessness when faced with the inferior system of education designed to perpetuate their second-class status as citizens. For years, I realised, that anger and frustration had been building up inside our young people – and the explosion, on 16 June 1976, had all the force of long-pent-up emotion. Ever since that date, South Africa has not been the same – and the days of passive resignation will never return to our land.

Part Two

Waiting at the Altar

Who is a wedding for? The bride? The groom? Or is it for all those guests who dress themselves in their finest for the day?

In close-knit communities, like the black communities of South Africa, a wedding has always been everybody's business, attracting prophets of doom, well-wishers and those who are simply curious. Whether the outcome is joyful or tragic, no one wants to be left out of the excitement.

Much is at stake for different people – the honour of the families, for example, and the continuation of community life. But those for whom the stakes are highest are the women to be married – the brides. For them, the wedding day marks the start of a new vulnerability.

The stories here show the public and private faces of two women's wedding days.

Life – a riddle

The wedding was a long-awaited event at the Thikgoma homestead. So, on the evening before, a large crowd was already present – talking in loud, joyous voices, darting this way and that with agile movements, and generally filling the air with jubilation and excitement.

Specially favoured members of the family were putting the finishing touches to the attire of the bride. Some were matching up the accessories – gloves, bouquet, earrings, necklace. Others were making sure that the bridesmaids' gowns were complete in every detail and ready to wear.

The remaining relatives had been assigned catering duties. These covered a great range of tasks, from planning the menu and making lists of items to be bought, to cooking and making salads and drinks for the day. And then there was the collecting of pots, dishes and cutlery from friends and family – a practice very common in the black community where sharing is a way of life.

Of course, many other arrangements had been made months in advance. Guests had been invited in good time and the programme for the day had been compiled. Entertainers had been engaged; a public venue had been booked for the evening festivities; a florist had been chosen to trim the hall. And the bride's family had discussed with the priest the order of the service and the kind of sermon he might like to preach.

The wedding – the focus of all these arrangements – was now close at hand and the evening was full of purposeful activity. Groups of young women sat peeling vegetables; while some of the older men were busy carving the slaughtered beasts. The older women were responsible for cleaning, washing and cooking the intestines of the animals and brewing the traditional beer. They had already been working on this last task for four or five days – that's how long the beer took to prepare.

On the whole, the younger generation looked on these chores as old-fashioned and uninteresting. They liked to see themselves as sophisticated – and this meant that they looked down on the traditions and customs of their culture, along with some of the values associated with it.

While all these tasks were being carried out around the homestead, the older members of the family remained in the house, discussing the wedding and everything connected with it.

The bride and her bridesmaids, meanwhile, were carrying out the tasks that needed their personal attention. Foremost in the bride's mind – and perhaps not that far distant from the thoughts of many people around and in the homestead – was an awareness that the bridegroom had not arrived on the 10 o'clock train as expected. But there was another train that night – at 12 o'clock; and the groom's sister assured the bride and her family that nothing would stop her brother arriving for the wedding.

The bride, though, was well aware that she had stiff competition from a rival – a woman who was on the scene before she herself met Bassie, her fiancé. Makie, the bride, recalled some of the disturbing and unkind remarks this woman had made when she first heard that Bassie was engaged to marry Makie. Makie had been on her way to work – she was a teacher in one of the local schools in Makeng – when she had the bad luck to meet Bassie's old girlfriend, Pusetso. The moment Pusetso recognised Makie, she came out with remarks like, 'Bassie will never marry anyone if he does not marry me,' and, 'Bassie will marry any other woman over my dead body.'

Several times after that, Makie had tried to raise the matter with Bassie, wanting to understand where he stood as regards Pusetso. But, each time, Bassie had discouraged Makie from discussing the subject. His closing remark on such occasions had always been, 'Makie, if I do not marry you, I will marry nobody else.' Makie had not felt wholly reassured by this remark.

Now, with her fiancé's arrival overdue, Makie turned these incidents and remarks over and over in her mind. And new thoughts constantly came to disturb her. There was, for example, the fact that Pusetso worked in the big city where Bassie had gone to have his wedding garments tailored. Makie knew only too well how daring and desperate Pusetso was. She would stop at nothing to win Bassie back – and might even harm him if she realised that she was fighting a losing battle. But Makie kept her thoughts and feelings to herself.

When Bassie failed to arrive on the 12 o'clock train, tension started to build up in all members of the two families. Members of the bride's family were particularly upset. They could hardly bear to think of the embarrassment, humiliation and scandal that they would suffer if no bridegroom appeared. For them, Bassie's failure to arrive could be interpreted as his rejection of them all – and that would count as a serious insult.

The jubilation and excitement that had carried the bride's family along for a week turned now into deep sorrow. Carefree laughter was replaced by soft weeping. The family could not bear to look their guests in the face. And so the mood changed everywhere in and around the homestead. The hopes of all the guests and helpers were dashed too. Where there had been loud, joyous voices, there were now sad, morose whispers; where there had been sprightly movements, there were now heavy, dragging steps. And the humming and singing which had filled the air were replaced by a sombre silence. Young and old alike seemed paralysed by unhappiness. People spoke only when they had to; and then their speech was in whispers.

As the night crept on, the bride could no longer prevent herself from crying uncontrollably, moaning and sighing. Her maids wept with her instead of comforting her. The whole atmosphere was more like that of a funeral than a wedding. Even the young bridesmaids appeared to have lost interest in their lovely gowns.

As relationships between the two families gradually grew sour, Bassie's eldest sister, who was heading her family group at the wedding, stepped in to try to prevent things getting even worse. She spoke to the women of her own age on the bride's side, comforted them and supported them as best she could. She showed great concern for the bride, who was by this time heavily sedated and under the constant care of the family doctor.

Bassie's sister then took some quick decisions. She summoned a meeting of the two families and reported to them that she intended to fetch her brother by hired car from the big city, about a hundred miles away. She would return with him early the next day. The wedding celebrations meanwhile must be postponed – but only by a day. The bride's family listened to her plans without enthusiasm; they had lost interest in the whole event. What she suggested sounded to them like compelling her brother to go through with the wedding when he had probably changed his mind. They were unconvinced when Bassie's sister put forward her strong belief that her brother had not changed his mind but had encountered a major problem.

In the end, Bassie's sister put aside all the family's arguments and objections. First, she got her brother on the phone. He tried to persuade her not to make the long journey; he would be arriving by train that night, he said. She replied firmly to this that she would arrive at his house to pick him up at such and such a time. And then she left for the long drive to the big city.

Back home at Fika-Tshetlha, life had almost come to a standstill. The pots which had been put on the fire that morning in preparation for the wedding feast stood on the hearth like mocking things. People were embarrassed to look at them. But, even though it was with unwilling hands, the helpers continued to prepare food and to cook.

The strong community spirit which marked the village kept the family's doors open to distant relatives and to neighbours. And, true to that spirit, these relatives and neighbours persuaded the bride's immediate family to allow them to take over all responsibility for the tasks and duties connected with the wedding celebrations. They worked hard at these tasks and, at the same time, did their best to raise the family's spirits.

The bride herself was looked after closely by one of her bridesmaids, Mpule, who was also her niece and confidante.

Eventually, Bassie's sister arrived at the place where he stayed – only to be told that he had left for the railway station to board a train to join his fiancée. His sister arrived at the station a few minutes before the train pulled out. Having spotted him, she got into his compartment, collected his luggage and bundled him into the car. She gave him no chance to explain anything. Within seconds, the car was on its way to Fika-Tshetlha.

As the hours dragged by, the family, guests and helpers grew increasingly uneasy and concerned about the arrival of the car. Most people doubted that the bridegroom would return with his sister. There were a number of prophets of doom whose loud and clear opinions created even more tension and anxiety in the home.

In their fear, hopelessness and disappointment, the bride's family started to plot against Bassie and his family. They tried to turn Makie against the man who was to have been her bridegroom. Temperatures ran very high, with remarks being exchanged like, 'He will never have the nerve to face us,' and, 'If he dares to do this to Makie before he marries her, what will he not do when they are husband and wife?' Another voice pronounced: 'Makie must just forget about Bassie – he is good for nothing.'

It was at the height of such exchanges – about half-past eight in the morning – that the black buick arrived. It crawled steadily towards the main gate of the homestead, with Bassie's sister sitting next to the driver and Bassie next to his sister, all of them on the front seat of the car. The arrival was met by whispered insults and curses from Makie's close relatives: they found it impossible to control their anger and disgust. As they watched Bassie step out of the car, they were ready to pounce on him with words – if not with fists.

To everybody's shock, Bassie got out of the car with a bewitching smile on his face. He was well-groomed, as usual, and had a quite unapologetic but polite air about him. He greeted the family in a composed and confident way and, as he shook hands with each member of the family in turn, the others looked on in stunned silence. No one had the courage to resist his handshake.

Bassie's manner changed, however, when he approached Makie's niece, Mpule. After shaking her hand, he asked in a trembling voice, 'Where is your aunt? How is she? Go, tell her I am here and would love to see her.' The questions and instructions tumbled out of him, giving the niece no chance to reply or to seek advice or permission from older relatives.

Mpule was shaken by doubt and fear. She looked at her relatives as if appealing for guidance or protection in the face of Bassie's command. When no word came, as if under a spell she dashed to the room where the bride was. Even then, not a single member of her family came forward. Without looking back, Mpule announced Bassie's arrival to Makie and told her that he was demanding to see her.

Before she had finished giving her report, there was a

gentle knock on the door. As Mpule opened the door, Bassie walked straight in. Mpule left immediately, Bassie closing the door behind her, with the sobbing of the bride ringing in her ears. In the time that followed, no relative approached the room. What transpired behind that closed door was only ever known to Makie and Bassie. No one – even from Makie's closest family – ever dared to ask.

In a mysterious way, Bassie's behaviour – defiant yet controlled – seemed to expel from the house the anger, mistrust and other evil emotions which had settled in such a heavy cloud before his arrival. Makie's family were completely taken aback. They had expected Bassie to conform to custom and tradition – which demanded from a son-in-law obedience and respect in relation to his in-laws. Bassie had disregarded all that was expected; but he had done so in an extremely polite and self-confident way. That situation left the family confused and helpless.

It was against this background that the families from both sides resumed plans and preparations for the wedding. It was like the wheels of a wagon being put back into motion. With renewed enthusiasm, the relatives and helpers at the Thikgoma homestead turned to their individual and collective tasks. And, once again, a feeling of joy and excitement spurred on their actions.

As if carried on a wild bush telegraph, word flew round the neighbourhood that the bridegroom had arrived and the wedding was on without any more delay, crowds grew and swelled. Some came on horseback, others in horse carts and carriages. Less well-to-do guests arrived on foot. Only a few came by car – these vehicles were far from common in the black community of those days. Like all major events, the occasion was not 'by invitation only'; all neighbours, near and far, were welcome.

Gaiety, swift movement and laughter broke up the earlier sombre mood. Heavy smoke from the hearth, where large pots of delicious food bubbled, announced far and wide that the long-awaited celebration was on.

The stable hands set to work grooming their horses and attaching the customary wedding trimmings to animals and carts in readiness for the procession to the church. Gradually, and at first reluctantly, the older members of the bride's family found themselves caught up in the spirit of excitement generated by the young people of both families. And then, in no time, best gowns, costumes and suits bought specially for the occasion were being discreetly paraded. All this added to the beauty and gay mood of the day.

At last, surrounded by singing crowds and piercing ululating, the bride emerged from her home with a confident step, followed by her brightly dressed bridesmaids – each of whom had a smile which stretched from one end of her cheek to the other. The poise and dignity with which the bridesmaids followed the bride, holding up the train of her wedding gown, made mockery of the incidents of the previous day. Proudly and confidently, they helped the bride up into the beautifully trimmed carriage.

Now, this was a magnificent affair indeed. And it was drawn by perfectly groomed stallions, each pepped up with a sip of brandy. Only the wealthy families of the community were able to travel in such style. The beasts were spirited, wagging their tails wildly, tossing their manes from side to side and stamping their impatient hooves. But they were soon brought under control by the steady hands of the seasoned driver. And, showing off with a jerk and a swift pull, he set the fine vehicle in motion.

Adorned with equally splendid trimmings, the other carts followed the procession to church. When it came to elegance of dressing, the passengers in each cart rivalled those who came before and after them. Ten to fifteen minutes after the carts had set out, the cars carrying the bridegroom and his party moved off.

The bridegroom's party were spellbound by the beauty

and agility of the horses, and admitted among themselves that such fine animals and carriages rather outshone any kind of motor car. The stallions seemed to these guests to be very steady and gentle – despite the effects of a tot of brandy. The bridegroom's family were accustomed to the antics of the inferior breed of horses and donkeys kept by their neighbours at home; in their part of the country, only rich white people kept the kind of horses they now saw. For their part, the bride's family took great pride in their horses; like their neighbours in the area, they looked on horses as the natural and accepted means of travel. And it was with great satisfaction that they observed the admiration and even envy displayed by the bridegroom's family.

As they travelled to the church, all the groups of guests discussed in hush-hush tones the events of the previous day. Although on the surface all was now well again, the uncertainty had left marks of pain and doubt. Many guests and relatives spoke quietly of their fears that the marriage would have a tragic end. All agreed that they could do nothing but 'wait and see'.

At the end of the ceremony, Bassie's relatives could hardly wait to escort the bride, proudly, to their sophisticated car, trimmed all over with colourful ribbons. Once several other cars had lined up behind, departure was announced by a variety of sounds. The cars hooted simultaneously, while the drivers encouraged women from the community to respond to the hoots by ululating in unison. The bride and the bridegroom had just settled comfortably in the car when it took off at full speed, followed by the others. Left behind was a thick cloud of dust from the untarred road of the country town.

With curses of, 'How dare they do this to us?' and, 'Surely they could have set off more gently?' and, 'How insensitive can they be?', the horse carts and carriages struggled to find their way through the dust cloud. The indignation of the bride's family aggravated their feeling of loss now that the bride had joined her husband. All the same, as they carried the rest of the guests back home, the drivers went to some pains to show off the paces of their beautiful and agile horses.

With the passing of time, Bassie became a well respected and loved son-in-law in the Thikgoma family, while Makie grew to be a respectable, mature and beloved daughter-in-law in Bassie's family. The prophets of doom proved to have a hard time of it, becoming more and more anxious and impatient as baby boys and girls arrived at planned intervals, as ripples of joy and laughter marked the new family's life, and as love and harmony bound together family and immediate relatives.

Fifty years after that unsettling day, long-forgotten, the couple, along with their six children and the rest of the immediate family, sent out invitations for the celebration of their Golden Jubilee.

A double dealer

During the early 1950s, Bonolo qualified as a schoolteacher. She was about twenty-five years of age and was a beautiful and elegant young woman; her garments always seemed to have been specially tailored for her well-proportioned figure. Every other man – of her own age and older – seemed to be attracted to her. All in all, she was the envy of the neighbourhood.

Bonolo's habitual manner of calm reserve put off many of these potential suitors. They found it much easier to approach girls who were less reserved about their feelings. But this same quality of quietness earned her many girlfriends. She had no special friend she was very close to; and yet all her friends seemed to be close to her.

Keeping herself very much to herself, Bonolo managed her time very well between leisure and duty, and appeared balanced and organised in her daily living. She gave the clear impression of a perfectly innocent young woman who knew what was good and right for her – and who lived accordingly.

Bonolo's private life was a closed book. She was not nasty to men. But she kept up friendships when they suited her and dismissed them when they became troublesome in some way. She begged neither men nor women for friendship; but when a hand of friendship was offered, she would take it without compromising herself in any way.

It was juicy news, then, when a rumour spread through

the neighbourhood that Bonolo was engaged to be married. The question everywhere was, 'Which man?' No amount of speculation could come up with the name of the lucky gentleman. Bonolo's friends, women and men alike, had many whispered discussions on the matter; but no one dared to ask Bonolo about him.

Like all rumours, this one was soon forgotten, overtaken by fresh gossip. And once the rumour dropped out of sight, people assumed that there had never been any truth in it in the first place. The fact that, unlike other girls of her age, Bonolo was never seen with one regular boyfriend strengthened the impression that the talk had been idle.

About a fortnight before the schools closed for the Christmas holidays, Bonolo started to distribute sealed envelopes to her friends and to her colleagues at work. Each recipient of an envelope was overwhelmed to discover that it was an invitation to Bonolo's wedding, to take place in a few weeks' time. The striking and unusual thing was that the bridegroom's name was unknown to all those who received an invitation. Even then, no one was brave enough to ask Bonolo who her fiancé was.

In the end, everyone decided to adopt a 'wait and see' attitude. But, of course, this did not mean there was any lack of hush-hush talk about the matter.

Each person invited to the event was determined to attend, whatever happened. And, knowing Bonolo's sense of style, all those invited to the wedding went out of their way to acquire fashionable clothes for the occasion, regardless of cost. Women and men alike, they were all keen to see this special man. Discussion of Bonolo's marriage often ended up with the comment, 'What a lucky man'.

On the Big Day, many of the guests – particularly the younger ones, friends and colleagues of Bonolo – decided to go straight to the church so that they could find seats with a good view of the proceedings. Every one of these young people was dressed up to the nines and in very good humour.

Most of the older guests were keen to go to the bride's home first, to join in the celebrations from beginning to end. There was a cool breeze but the day was bright and glowing with sunshine. Some guests stood in small groups, chatting, while others sat down in chairs spread around the colourful marquee which had been pitched beside the main house. The rest relaxed on the verandah, talking and laughing.

Among the guests in the marquee was a middle-aged woman, reasonably well dressed but with a less fashionable appearance than many others of her age. She had a toddler by the hand and was accompanied by a boy of about ten years of age and a younger girl of about seven. While everybody around her sat chatting and laughing, she seemed preoccupied with the rather restless youngsters in her charge. The woman, who seemed to be the mother of the children, showed some signs of anxiety.

There was no doubt that the woman was a stranger in the neighbourhood. No one seemed to know her and no one even made a move to speak to her. She was one of the few people who had arrived at the marquee almost an hour before it was time to leave for the church. She occupied a seat which exposed her to all who entered and left the house and the marquee; and, despite the fact that her children were getting bored with sitting in the same place, she seemed determined to keep that seat.

Eventually, the two older children got very restless indeed: they needed to be accompanied to the closet. Luckily, a young girl in the crowd noticed her plight and offered to take the two children. The woman must have been grateful for the offer, since the girl's help allowed her to retain that well-placed seat.

About thirty minutes before the time of departure for the church, a jubilant roar set up outside the marquee and there was the sound of people moving about. This was accompanied by traditional ululating from the women of the community who jumped and danced while holding brooms in a kind of sweeping motion – one of the many ways of welcoming a bridal party into the home. The crowd began to swell and close in on the groom and his retinue as they arrived to meet the bride and her bridesmaids. The seated guests grew restless: they half wanted to keep their seats and half wanted to go out to see the bridegroom enter. Some stood up – but shouts of, 'Please sit down', and, 'You're blocking our view', soon made them resume their seats. The situation showed signs of becoming chaotic.

At that point, a firm order was given – that all those with seats should sit down in order to give the bridal party room to move in and out of the marquee. Like all the other guests, the strange woman obeyed the announcement and kept her seat facing the door.

In an atmosphere of great excitement, marked by constant ululating and singing, the groom's party waited outside to meet the bride's party. The woman had some difficulty in keeping her two older children sitting quietly beside her, carried away as they were by the general mood of hilarity.

Suddenly, the door which faced her chair opened and the bridegroom and his party made their entrance. All eyes turned that way. The bridegroom lifted his head high – and immediately met the gaze of the woman sitting there opposite the door. He went pale with shock. The boy was about to jump up when his mother caught him by the shoulder and held him down, telling him to stay where he was. He obeyed, looking bewildered.

Within seconds, the groom turned to his first best man, whispering something to him as he held his tummy tight, as if in great pain. He started to perspire and stagger and the rest of his best men, supporting him from falling down, helped him to move out of sight. It was guessed that he was taken to the car hired to convey the bride and her groom from home to church.

Soon word passed around the crowd that the bridegroom had suddenly been taken ill and was in a serious condition.

There was general confusion, panic and distress. By that time, the bride was fully dressed, ready to go before the priest to say 'I do'. She was traumatised to learn of her bridegroom's unexpected illness. She wept uncontrollably and all efforts to comfort her failed. She refused to believe the accounts given to her of what had happened. To whatever was said to her, she replied, 'The only person I want now is Leruo.' Leruo was, of course, the man she was about to marry.

Shaken by these events, Bonolo's family moved quickly to see what help could be given to their future son-in-law. While they were busy arranging for him to be taken to the doctor, they were shocked to discover that Leruo had suddenly disappeared with his best man, leaving no trace.

In all the commotion and tumult, the strange woman and her three children had slipped out from the house – leaving unnoticed and unannounced, just as they had arrived. A buzz of talk started up about who they were, where they came from and how they came to be at the house. Someone said, 'They must have gone home.' Another then asked, 'Where *is* home?' But no one had an answer to that. They had come and they had gone and that was that.

Following on that, the joyous mood of the day had turned into chaos, hurt and bitterness. The bride was in tears and on the brink of collapse. She was quickly taken away to the doctor and from there to hospital. The rest of the family stayed at home, trying to solve and understand the mystery of the bridegroom's sudden illness and disappearance.

Word soon reached the crowd in church that something tragic had happened at the bride's home. Filled with curiosity, everyone rushed there to get the story at first hand. On their arrival, they added to the confusion and soon became even more muddled themselves about the events of the day.

The guests stood in groups around the house, gossiping. At one point, someone aroused people's curiosity by referring to the sudden disappearance of 'a strange woman with three children'. Someone else laughing, asked, 'Was she a witch?' Some people in this group joined in the laughter; but others criticised the speaker for making unkind remarks at a time of such difficulty and distress. In every corner of the homestead, different groups were asking the same questions – 'Who was the strange woman?', 'Where has she gone to?', 'How did she come here?' and, 'When did she leave?' In a state of high excitement, they were really only talking for the sake of talking: no one expected a reply or was able to give one. But now and then, the remark could be heard repeated: 'She is a witch.'

After about an hour, the crowd of guests and family began to break up. Some of the family remained to discuss what should be done next, while others took their turn watching over the bride at the hospital. The guests meanwhile departed in small groups, many of them faced with long journeys home.

The events of that day left a bitter taste with all those who had been there. For days on end, the talk in the immediate neighbourhood was of nothing else. And then, within a fortnight, the mystery was solved. The local paper appeared with the headlines:

MARRIED MAN ON SECOND WEDDING CELEBRATION
Wife and children turn tables on wedding day

For all the wedding guests, the pieces of the jigsaw then fell into place. The 'bridegroom', known to all as 'a real double dealer', went back to his parents' home in utter shame. His wife, a mother of three, called a witch that day, then started to fend for herself and her children. She had lost all trust in her husband, who had lived with her up to the day of the 'wedding'. What had happened, it turned out, was that on that day he pretended to be going to the seaside with his employers. But by then his wife had heard of his plans to 'marry' another woman and to move to a far-off city.

As for Bonolo, she never wanted to see the man again after that traumatic experience. She went into a mental depression and has never recovered to this day. She lost her girlhood charm, her calm, reserved manner, her ability to make and keep friends. Her attractive appearance, which charmed young men, became a thing of the past. Her casual smile was replaced by a perpetual frown and a sour expression. Her head, which used to be held so high, drooped down. She lost her sprightly walk. Later, she did make a 'real' marriage – but she remained sour, unhappy, unfriendly and friendless.

Part Three

What is a Family?

In a society like South Africa where state welfare systems offer very little to those who are poor or in trouble, the family means much more than simply the giving and taking of love and support – it often makes the difference between a person being able to survive and not being able to survive.

The importance of the family in the black community is matched only by the complexity of the relationships that may be involved. During this century, as the four stories here illustrate, Christian, western and traditional ideas have all contributed to our concept of marriage and the family – and they have at times clashed headlong. On top of this, we have suffered badly from the disintegration of our traditional values caused by the drift of people to the big cities in search of work. Once there, legal and other constraints have put great pressure on people's ability to live ordered and decent lives. Migrant labour regulations have added to these hardships.

Even in rural areas, white interference in black people's lives is never far distant. In the story 'One of many', for example, the young man, Mosa, becomes the indirect victim of the government's practice of forced removals. Until you have first hand experience of such removals, it is impossible to understand the emotional and physical trauma involved. These removals are never negotiated with the residents of a community. If there are negotiations, they are generally between the authorities and those whom the authorities regard as the representatives of the state – a 'Headman' or a 'Chief', specially selected by the government. Such negotiations are usually followed by an announcement giving the date of the removal.

At first, residents resist the removal. This resistance creates great tension – which often ends up with a police charge. Dogs are used and there is shooting. All kinds of force are brought to bear on the residents in order to intimidate them into co-operating with the removal. The most distressing stage is when the residents see their houses bulldozed and their furniture and household items violently flung about the place. Eventually, the residents have to face up to being physically removed from where they lived, along with the few possessions that they managed to save. Some residents give in at this stage; but others still refuse to leave. Many residents have lost their lives in such struggles. For those who do leave, it is only later that the reality of having no home, no land, no fields to plough sinks in. The frustration, helplessness and depression that follow are beyond what can be imagined or adequately described.

This removal of black communities from the land they owned had a large number of far-reaching effects. One of these was the decline in the traditional practice of polygamy (and many other cultural standards), the subject of 'The reward of waiting'. This practice was recognised and respected until, perhaps, the 1930s. But as black people were deprived of their livestock, husbands could no longer afford the *lobola* (bride price) that was a necessary indication of the status of the wife. At the same time, women's growing desire, particularly in the cities, to make their own mark in economic and educational terms led to considerable resistance to this traditional practice.

As Christianity and its values took root in the black community and as more and more people embraced education and the kind of new work opportunities which arose, large numbers of black people began to move away from polygamy, seeing it as un-Christian and uncivilised. Those who still clung to it as a cultural norm defended it partly as an effective measure for spacing births. While a new mother was nursing her baby, the husband lived with the other wife. Thus, the new mother had time to recuperate and care for her baby without being disturbed by her husband's desire for sexual intercourse.

Polygamy was also seen as a source of economic security for a family. The different wives were each allocated a piece of land which they tilled and cultivated for different crops depending on the season. Each wife was thus able to meet the needs of her own children. In later years, when the black community was dispossessed of its land through the colonial laws of South Africa, the children of individual families represented economic security. This was particularly true where the family lived on land owned by white farmers who depended on cheap black labour. When the parents grew old, they could only remain on this land because of the labour contracts of their children. Sons were always looked on as a safer security because, according to custom and tradition, on the son's marriage he and his new wife would live with or near his parents. Daughters, on the other hand, were considered a security risk because, after marriage, they left home to live with their husband's family.

Education – no substitute for culture

Outside the small country town of Nkweng stood a dilapidated village of black people. There were a few modern homes owned by educated people – teachers, nurses, ministers of religion, health inspectors, and so on. But most of the villagers could barely read or write and were very poor.

Because their situation was so much better than that of their neighbours, the educated families and individuals tended to think a great deal of themselves. Indeed, some families went so far as to despise the traditional values and customs of their own people. They tried to ape other race groups and seemed to prefer the values of those groups to their own. This way of thinking and behaving helped to undermine further the morale of the villagers who had missed out on any opportunities for education or money-making.

Mr Piet Kgosi's family was part of this upper stratum of the community. Piet and his wife, Annie, were both schoolteachers. The husband came from the second generation of teachers in his family. The wife was the first generation in her family. Piet recognised fully that his achievement was a family group effort. Without the support and contribution of his family – and of his sister in particular – he knew he could never have become a schoolteacher. With that fact constantly in his mind, he was always determined to give help in his family when it was needed, especially where schooling was concerned.

Piet was deeply upset when his sister died young, a single parent leaving behind a son who was two years older than Piet's oldest child. Taking a secret vow, he pledged himself to see his sister's son through high school at least and to help him all he could to get settled at work and have a family of his own. Piet was sure that that would be the proper way to thank his sister for all the sacrifices she had made for his education – an established tradition in the black communities of South Africa. So Piet brought his sister's son, Thulo, into his family, accepting him as his oldest child.

It soon became clear that his wife did not approve of this decision. She did not openly express her resentment of Thulo; but she was not kind to the boy.

Twelve years old when his mother died, Thulo now had his maternal uncle (*malome*) as his sole guardian. From his early childhood, Thulo had always been attached to his uncle, the only adult male in the family, the head of the family being Piet's mother, Thulo's grandmother. For Thulo, Piet was both uncle and 'father'. And Thulo meant to his uncle what his uncle meant to him. They were inseparable, and continued to be so despite Annie's hostility.

Piet was determined to give his nephew all the love, care and support he needed. That was foremost in his mind. He gave him constant moral support and, in addition to this, often made time to speak to him in confidence about the difficult family situation. 'Thulo,' he would say, 'I recognise that you carry a heavy load of duties in my home, without help from other members of the family and without any word of appreciation. Be that as it may, I plead with you – take it all in good spirit for the sake of your education and your overall future. I promise to be by your side at all times.' The uncle would conclude, 'Even in my silence I will always support you.'

Thulo's response to his uncle was always, '*Malome*, it is

very difficult, but I will try my best at all times.' Piet would then thank the boy – the only time Thulo ever heard a word of thanks in the family.

Thulo had a gruelling routine from the time he was twelve until the time he was eighteen and left high school. After waking up, he would make the fire and serve morning tea to the other members of the family – they were still in bed. Then he would heat up water so that the family could wash themselves; prepare a light breakfast; clean and tidy certain areas of the house. And, finally, he would get ready for school. On his return from school, he would immediately finish cleaning the house. Then he would attend to the washing and ironing of the family's clothes. Next was work in the garden. His domestic tasks were rounded off by washing the dishes after supper while the rest of the family relaxed round the table, chatting. After that, he would turn to his school work.

Piet took a firm stand that his child should help Thulo with the domestic tasks. But Annie paid little attention to this. Instead she indirectly encouraged the children to leave the tasks to Thulo alone. For example, after supper, she would tell them to stay at the table and do their homework.

Piet soon found himself in a dilemma. He was torn between wanting to take his nephew to live elsewhere and the desire to bring up his children and his nephew under the same roof. It was the latter wish that finally got the upper hand; but Piet continued to drift along from day to day, making up his mind and then changing it again.

This way of life weighed heavily on Piet and took a good deal out of him. As well as his concern for Thulo, there was the question of the upbringing of his own children. He was very hurt to see his daughter grow up untrained and unprepared for her responsibilities in the home. Other mothers, he could see, were grooming their daughters to be all-rounders when they reached maturity. But, at the àge of ten, Dikgopi, his daughter, still depended on Thulo to wash her socks and panties – a shameful thing in the black community.

Thulo survived his ordeal. He finished at high school and went on to train as a policeman – a period of another two years. He continued living with his uncle's family – and continued to endure harsh treatment from his aunt.

His uncle and aunt had three children, two boys and then a girl. By the time Thulo started his training in the police, Moji, the eldest, had enrolled at the university to take a diploma in agricultural demonstration. Annie could not stop telling people about this brilliant son of hers. Tshepo, the younger son, had always been close to Thulo and, perhaps out of solidarity, he too began to train as a policeman. Dikgopi had never shown much interest in school; and, at the age of sixteen, her schooling came to an abrupt end when she found that she was expecting a baby.

Piet's health was now beginning to decline; and this weighed very heavily on Thulo. He could not imagine life in that home without his uncle. But no alternative would be possible for him: he was still in the middle of his studies and therefore had no chance of starting his own family. Thulo prayed in silence for his uncle's recovery. These prayers were not answered in full since Piet remained ill. But Thulo was consoled to see his uncle manage from day to day, even though he was an invalid and out of work. During this time, Piet managed to maintain Thulo and the rest of his family out of his meagre savings.

Thulo was very happy when he was able to finish his training as a policeman and find a job while his uncle was still alive. With his limited earnings, Thulo did all in his power to reduce the financial burden carried by his uncle. For example, he made a major contribution towards buying groceries for the family. There was no doubt that Annie recognised and appreciated Thulo's contribution towards the family expenditure; yet she never got round to expressing her gratitude, either directly or through her husband.

In due course, Thulo took a transfer from Nkweng to work at Majweng, where he was immediately promoted to a senior position. That promotion gave him the opportunity to save and make his plans for marriage a reality. This development was a great relief to his uncle, who was very keen to see Thulo get married while he could still give him some help in setting up his home.

Piet's health took a surprising change for the better. This gave him the opportunity to respond to Thulo's marriage as fully as he wished, carrying out all the duties as guardian and more. One other matter of importance that gave Piet great joy was to see the strong bond of friendship between Thulo and Tshepo both in their employment and at home.

Three months after Thulo's wedding, Piet's health deteriorated. Shortly afterwards, he died peacefully. It was a great loss to the whole family, but especially to Thulo who lost an uncle, a 'father', a friend and a rare confidant. 'I felt my road had come to a dead stop,' he said later.

At the time, the only member of the family who showed him warmth and affection was Tshepo, the cousin who was in the police force with him. As if in response to Thulo's loss of his uncle, Tshepo seemed determined to keep very close to Thulo; in fact, he was hardly willing to let Thulo out of his sight. Of course, Thulo noticed this unusual behaviour and gently tried to tell Tshepo that he need not be so intense; but Tshepo was not to be put off. The result of all this was that the two cousins became closer than ever.

Tshepo would often ask Thulo to accompany him when he went to Nkweng to visit his family; and, despite the fact that he was reluctant to go, Thulo found it impossible to turn down an invitation extended by his cousin. But Thulo made a vow never to take his wife back to his family home. He gave his wife no reasons for this decision; he simply refused to take her to Nkweng whenever he went there with Tshepo. Tshepo, of course, was able to read between the lines and understand why Thulo took this stand; and he did not pursue the matter any further. But this did not have a harmful effect on the relationship between the cousins. On the contrary, they grew closer by the day – at work, in their leisure time and at family events. This was a great puzzle for Annie, but she found it impossible to probe into the matter.

On one particular weekend, the cousins planned to make a visit to Nkweng. There had been a gap of five or six weeks since their last visit because their off-duty times had not coincided. At the last minute, Thulo was assigned to stand in for a senior official who had been taken ill and was in hospital. Realising that it had been a long time since their last visit to Nkweng, the cousins decided that Tshepo should make the trip in the company of some of their colleagues who also came from the village. To avoid unnecessary expense, all the men were to travel in one car.

Thulo and Tshepo clubbed together to buy groceries for Annie. They parted at Thulo's house on the Friday evening when the car came to pick up Tshepo. They said their good-byes only after their colleagues had remonstrated about their 'endless family talks'. Just before the car pulled off, one of the men jokingly remarked, 'Tshepo, you must find a girl-friend and stop clinging to your cousin-brother like a cissy!'

At six o'clock the next morning, the police station tele-phone rang with a call for Thulo. When he replied, he thought he recognised the voice of one of his colleagues who had left with Tshepo the day before. He was right. What was the news? Trembling and mumbling, the colleague's voice said something about a car accident and about Tshepo. In a panic, Thulo said, 'Please repeat your message. I did not get it.' There was dead silence, except for heavy breathing and the indistinct sound of someone sobbing. A fellow worker standing beside Thulo recognised the panic on his face and took the receiver from him. 'Please let me know who is speaking,' he said, firmly and clearly. The reply came in a feeble voice, 'Thabo.' 'Thabo,' said the fellow worker, 'what is the message you have for Thulo?' Dead silence for a few seconds, then came a reply, 'Modise, is that you?' 'Yes, it is I. Is there anything wrong?' asked Modise. 'Yes, very wrong. Our car skidded in a heavy downpour when we were on the road approaching Nkweng, about one hundred and fifty kilometres before we reached the town. It overturned. I got out with minor scratches and a pain in my back. Toko is admitted to hospital in the intensive care unit. And I am sorry to report that Tshepo died in that accident.'

By this time, many policemen from different offices had crowded into the office where Thulo worked, all waiting to hear what had happened. Thulo sat on a chair nearby, his head buried in his hands which rested on the table. Even before he heard the full report of the accident, his shoulders heaved as he gave out very moving sobs.

Senior officers moved forward to take Thulo to the sick-bay, to explain to him what had happened, and to give him the support he needed. The reality of Tshepo's death soon hit Thulo. His last hope, beloved cousin-brother, friend and confidant. The young man who had replaced his uncle-father. He whispered to himself, 'I am left alone in this cold, harsh world.'

When he had got over his first shock, he went straight to the clinic where his wife worked to tell her of the tragedy that had befallen the family. He then made arrangements for his absence for seven to ten days. He seemed like a completely broken man. His wife, Manana, had known Tshepo well – and also knew what he meant to Thulo. The implications of his death, along with the shock itself, overwhelmed her and she too broke down. Fortunately, those in charge of the clinic allowed her to go home.

After making the necessary arrangements for Manana to travel to Nkweng to attend the funeral the following Friday, Thulo left for the family home to help with the funeral plans and all else that needed to be done. The family broke down at their first sight of Thulo. The fact that Thulo and Tshepo had always come together to this home had a very painful touch for Piet's family. For the first time, they displayed an attachment to Thulo; this was new, strange and awkward for him. All the same, he accepted it without comment. There was no doubt that Annie was destroyed by Tshepo's death.

In the days that followed, Thulo stood by his uncle's family as he always did. His wife came to Nkweng for the first time since they were married. She arrived three days before the funeral and took her place immediately as the senior and only 'daughter-in-law' in her husband's uncle's home – the only place her husband could call 'home'. As she took over the running of the house, Manana displayed outstanding qualities of efficiency and sensitivity. The great emotional burdens being carried by the members of the family seemed to bring out the best in her. She comforted the family, allocated duties, made arrangements, all the time working side by side with her husband. While they worked, Thulo explained to her the position and standing of each family member as they arrived in order to avoid the kinds of misunderstandings or difficulties that tend to happen at family events. This effort was worthwhile: at the end of the funeral, there were very few complaints from the many members of the family present.

When it came time for Manana to leave, Annie and her children expressed their gratitude and appreciation for all she and Thulo had done. They thanked Manana in particular – coming for the first time into the family at such a sensitive and sad moment. Annie's last words to Manana were, 'Manana, don't forget us. Remember you have a home in Nkweng too.' To which she replied, 'I will come and see you soon, Aunt Annie.' Tears were streaming down the cheeks of all the members of the family in that room, women and men alike. The family parted with sobs, moaning and great distress. Thulo remained behind for a few days as he needed to discuss with his aunt the procedures for making the insurance claims.

By this time, Annie seemed like a different person. Her arrogance, cold-blooded meanness and unfairness were fast thawing away. It was unbelievable. She sat on her verandah in her pitch-black mourning outfit, which covered her from head to foot, watching relatives and friends leave her homestead. There was no doubt that the wound she had suffered was even deeper than people had supposed. Her daughter Dikgopi, on the other hand, appeared untouched by the pain that afflicted the rest of the family. And Moji, the elder son, kept asking his mother about when and how she was going to claim the insurance money – a subject which at that point seemed to be far from his mother's mind.

It was with great interest, then, that Moji joined in the discussions on procedures for claiming the insurance money. However, Dikgopi immediately distanced herself from all that. Every time the family gathered to discuss issues arising from Tshepo's death, they tried to persuade Dikgopi to be present. But, on the times when she came, she made no comment, even when her opinion was sought. It was difficult to fathom her thoughts. She was cold and indifferent, holding herself aloof from the family. She relaxed with strangers and spoke to them easily – but not to her own family. Her behaviour was very odd.

Once the preliminary work had been done on the insurance claims, Thulo left for Majweng. He promised his aunt that he would keep in touch and, for the first time since his uncle's death, he left his phone number so that his aunt could contact him if she needed him. Thulo's departure was like the last straw for the family. Even Dikgopi broke down completely when he left. She took him to the taxi rank and seemed very unwilling to leave him. As the taxi was about to pull off, she whispered into Thulo's ear, 'I am sure going to leave this home soon, to find work in the big city.' Thulo's reply to that was, 'Don't be silly, Dikgopi. You must be by Aunt Annie's side and keep her company.' They said their goodbyes as the taxi began to move.

As Tshepo had still been a bachelor, his mother received all the insurance benefits linked to his employment. Moji got very excited when he heard how much money his mother was to receive. Annie was taken aback by this shameful reaction; for her, no money could replace Tshepo. She was embarrassed and angered by Moji's attitude. And, even after all the money had been paid into her account, Annie remained indifferent to it. Nothing seemed to comfort, support or cheer Annie after her son's death. No. Nothing. The two children who remained with her clearly did not make up for the loss.

Moji went back to his work as an agricultural demonstrator almost a month after his younger brother's funeral. He had found every possible excuse for not going back; but his mother finally pushed him back to work. Dikgopi's attention was focused on her baby, who was about a year old. She was very unwilling to respond in any way to requests or instructions from her mother. Only under pressure from relatives would she make her mother a cup of tea or prepare her breakfast. She was very unco-operative at all levels. She made food for herself and her child only. If Moji asked for anything from her, she ignored him.

For about a year, Annie suffered acutely from the pain of her son's death. Meanwhile, she had to endure unmanageable behaviour from her two remaining children. They were very different from Tshepo, who had been the replica of his father in physique and manner. No doubt many things came back to Annie. She must have recalled, in particular, her husband's warnings and reprimands about her way of bringing up the children.

The last straw came when Dikgopi told her mother that she was going to the big city to find a job and that she was taking her child with her. All the pleas from her mother not to go fell on deaf ears. Annie realised that even if she phoned Thulo about Dikgopi's plans, it would not help – Majweng was miles away from the big city. She must also have thought of the way she had ill-treated Thulo and protected and pampered her own children at his expense. She ended up by suffering in silence. But she did at least succeed in persuading Dikgopi to leave the baby with her. This was the only piece of advice Dikgopi took from her mother.

Eighteen months after Tshepo's death, his mother's health began to decline. Few relatives were able to come in to help with household chores and with nursing. There had been heavy rains, and the residents of the village, Annie's relatives among them, had to work hard ploughing the fields. More and more messages were sent to Dikgopi, telling her to come back home to help nurse and care for her mother. Word was also sent to Thulo, giving him his cousin's address and asking him to contact her with a view to persuading her to return. Having failed to get a reply from Dikgopi, Thulo finally went to the big city to trace her. And, having found her, he took her home under escort to nurse her mother. Annie died within a fortnight of Dikgopi's return.

Thulo and Manana joined the family in burying Annie, who was then the oldest person in Piet's home. She was given a decent burial – signifying forgiveness for all her shortcomings during the early years when she was a young mother and a senior woman in the family. Once again, Thulo was the one who ran the event. And the family was only too happy to have Manana to help. Except for the tiffs she had with Moji, Dikgopi was quite co-operative on this occasion. She agreed to stay in Nkweng for at least two months after her mother's burial, looking after the home and packing whatever needed to be collected and stored.

The family was reasonably happy when they left for their different homes. When Thulo and Manana left, they told Moji and Dikgopi to get in touch with them if they needed help. Relationships within the family at the time of parting were warm, comforting and encouraging. Everyone was pleasantly surprised by the goodwill and co-operation from

Dikgopi. She seemed determined to look after the home properly for the time that she remained there.

About a fortnight later, Manana received a phone call from Dikgopi, requesting her to please ask Thulo to come to Nkweng over the weekend, as soon as he could make it. Thulo agreed to go; but as he did not think it urgent, he put it off for a fortnight. The next telephone call from Dikgopi was directed to Thulo. She pleaded with him to get to Nkweng as soon as possible.

There was now no doubt in Thulo's mind that there was something wrong in Nkweng, needing urgent attention. He went there the next weekend. On his arrival on the Friday evening, there was no sign of trouble. Dikgopi welcomed him and, without saying much, allowed him to retire. He barely noticed Moji's absence from home on the evening, dismissing it as the usual behaviour of young men of Moji's age. He did not even remark on it to Dikgopi.

Thulo was up early the next day, taking a walk round the homestead and thinking of the 'good old days'. Suddenly, he saw Moji stealthily coming through the back gate – coming home at six o'clock in the morning. Moji was taken aback to see Thulo. Bewildered by the sight of him, Moji walked straight up to his cousin and, without greeting him, started making accusations against Dikgopi. 'Yes, I know she phoned you to come and catch me out. Dikgopi is awful. She must get married. I am the master of this home. I do what pleases me now.' Thulo stood there, perplexed but now aware of why he had been summoned to Nkweng. Before Thulo could respond, Moji continued, 'Tell me now why you are here.' Without saying a word, Thulo left him standing there and continued his walk as if untouched by the confrontation. Moji disappeared into the house and went to his bedroom.

After breakfast, at about ten o'clock, the relatives who knew Thulo was coming arrived to welcome him and to start the family discussion. Thulo could not stop marvelling at Dikgopi: the dignified way she carried herself; the way she maintained the home; the manner in which she received the guests. All this showed a great change in her. Thulo turned to her, saying, 'Thank you for everything, cousin.' Smiling, Dikgopi replied, '*Motsoala* (cousin), who can live with Manana and not copy her? You have chosen a wonderful wife for us.'

After thanking Dikgopi for her kind words, Thulo thanked the relatives present for all they had done – in particular for the moral and material support they were giving to Dikgopi and Moji. On the relatives' faces, he could see the approval when he mentioned Dikgopi and the indifferent reaction when he mentioned Moji. All the same, he pretended to notice nothing. He then remarked, 'The only person I am missing now is *motsoala* Moji.' No one responded. Dikgopi stood up, saying, 'I will check in his bedroom.' She had been gone about five minutes when she returned, followed by Moji. He was acceptable in appearance but subdued and still not altogether sober. 'Good morning,' Moji said. The family responded unanimously with, '*Dumela* (good morning), Moji.'

Without any waste of time, the oldest man on Piet's side of the family related their concern about Moji's irresponsible behaviour. He informed Thulo that in recent weeks, Moji had put in only irregular appearances at work; and that he abused Dikgopi, particularly when he had liquor – a daily occurrence. Their greatest worry lay in the fact that Dikgopi was threatening to go back to the big city if Moji continued to behave in this way. When this senior member of the family had finished his report, Thulo asked Moji to respond to the allegations.

On his feet, disregarding all those present, old and young, Moji turned on Dikgopi, accusing her of making unfounded statements about him. He openly declared how much he wanted to see Dikgopi leave the home. He shouted out that all the other girls of her age were married and that, by now,

Dikgopi should be running a home of her own, well away from the house that was his. Moji became so hysterical that he would not listen to reason from the relatives there in that room. It was certainly clear to all those present that Moji did not want his sister living with him in their common home.

In his usual cool and collected manner, Thulo spoke to Moji, asking him to finish what he was saying so that the family could come to a conclusion about his allegations. Looking puzzled by Thulo's cool manner, Moji sat up straight, as if waking from a dream. Thulo then turned to Dikgopi, saying, 'You heard all that Moji said, Dikgopi. What is your response?' Dikgopi responded calmly, 'I am in this house because' – here, she pointed at the family – 'you requested me to remain in this home for at least two months, looking after it. Now that you are witnesses to what has been said, I have decided to leave Moji and his home. I am going back to the big city.'

The relatives begged Dikgopi to remain at Nkweng; but they failed to persuade her to do so. She went back to the big city, and there she met a man who offered her his hand in marriage. Her husband accepted the child she brought with her and, in due course, they were blessed with three children of their own. Dikgopi and Kgotso, her husband, lived with Kgotso's mother, who owned a house in the black township of the big city. Dikgopi was very fortunate to find herself in a home marked by love, warmth, caring and peaceful commitment to daily living. And Dikgopi's family were very happy to see her adjust to that way of life. Now she would make a success of things, they felt sure.

Nine years later, word came to her family that she had gone back to her old habits; her upbringing had caught up with her. She had started to behave in an irresponsible way – staying away from her employment, not coming home for days on end, and leaving her old mother-in-law with the whole responsibility of running the home and looking after the children. She was squandering her earnings and had the audacity to go to her husband's place of work to demand money from him. The wonder of it all is that her husband did not end their marriage.

Dikgopi ended up as a wanderer, a prostitute, and someone who seemed beside herself. She never ventured to go near Nkweng or to visit her cousin Thulo's house. In fact, she ignored or rejected the many invitations that Thulo and his family sent her – although they were never sure how many of these invitations she received since had no fixed abode. She thus ended up lost to herself and to her family. She became a true example of a child brought up with foreign, unfounded concepts of culture and tradition.

Shortly after Dikgopi's departure from Nkweng, Moji left his job as an agricultural demonstrator. He concentrated instead on winding up his mother's estate. That done, he began to live the life of a very irresponsible 'squire'. Close and distant relatives tried all in their power to advise and guide Moji. But their efforts were all in vain. He bought very expensive clothes. He was driven in a lavish car by a chauffeur. He drank expensive liquor in the company of an exclusive class of women – women without scruples. He became the talk of the town and the envy of fools. Every man in the community became his 'friend'. He took up the empty, cheap slogans of city drunkards – 'Fill up the table, count the bottles and collect your cash'.

Those who had his welfare at heart were very upset by his self-indulgence. But they could do nothing about it. Within a year, there came the first signs of bankruptcy. His company of men and women was on the decline. He began to walk the streets occasionally – and sometimes to drive his own car. Soon the rumour went round that Moji was beginning to sell the household furniture – then the odd utensils in the home. The last straw was when he sold the house itself. It was not long before he became homeless, destitute and altogether unwanted by his old 'friends'.

Moji ended up as a herdboy for families far below the rank

of his own family in its heyday. But his health soon let him down. He developed a very depressing physical condition, with swelling knees and legs. His story resembles in many ways the biblical story of the prodigal son. But with one major difference – Moji never had the opportunity to ask forgiveness from his parents. Once again, in the end Thulo had to step in. When Moji became very ill and bedridden, Thulo took him back to his home in Majweng; and, before very long, he buried him from there.

In her folly, Annie had abused Thulo, in the full belief that she loved her own children. But she never taught them the basics of self-respect, responsibility, duty, respect for others and common courtesy. Her children were never introduced to their own black culture or taught to value it.

One of many

Mosa, a young boy, was very precious to his mother, Mpho. They lived with Mpho's family on the out-skirts of the small town of Nukastel, on a white farmer's land. According to today's standards, Mpho was a single parent. As Mosa was her first and only child, they were very close to each other. Altogether, it was a warm family and a happy one.

When Mosa was about ten years old, his mother developed a relationship with Jabu, a man in his middle thirties and older than Mpho. As their friendship matured, the two began to discuss the possibility of marriage.

Mpho loved Jabu; but she felt unable to accept his hand in marriage without a guarantee that he would have no hesi-tation in accepting both herself and her child into his family. In the traditional setting, a marriage is not just the concern of the bride and bridegroom. The two immediate families are also deeply involved at all levels of arrangement and planning, and in some instances even in daily living. It was because of this that Mpho felt strongly that Jabu's family must state explicitly that Mosa would be accepted into the family as their child. In some cases, if children come with their mothers into a marriage, the price of the *lobola* paid for their mothers is raised. In such cases, the children automati-cally take the family name of their stepfather.

In her concern about the future of her son after her

marriage to Jabu, Mpho turned to her mother for guidance. She was well aware that her mother loved Mosa, her oldest grandchild, very much indeed. In their talk about this sensitive subject, Mpho's mother, without weighing her words, asked her daughter, '*Mma-Mosa ngoanaka* (Mosa's mother, my child), do you want me to believe that you have always entertained the idea that some day, when you find a husband and a home you can call your own, you would take Mosa along with you?'

Bewildered by her mother's question, Mpho replied in all sincerity, 'Mother, my brother is married – and he has his wife and children to care for. I hate to burden him with the upbringing of my son; Mosa is my responsibility. And my brother also has you to look after. I have told Jabu in no uncertain terms that, if he truly loves me, he cannot hope to have me without my son. He has accepted that.'

With great seriousness, Mpho's mother reminded her daughter of custom and tradition in such a matter. She pointed out that, for generations, the black community had laid it down almost as law that a child born out of wedlock belongs to his or her maternal uncle's family – in other words, the mother's family – and remains a member of that family when the mother decides to get married to another man. In a firm voice, Mpho's mother then asked her, 'How can you disregard a practice so established and accepted by your community?'

Mpho collected herself to reply to her mother, her lips trembling and her eyes glossy with tears. But her mother continued, 'Why do you think we all rallied round when Mosa was born, feeding, clothing and nursing both of you with so much love?' Still her mother gave Mpho no chance to speak. 'We did that because we accepted him as our very own. What do you think your father will think of me in his grave if I allowed you to take Mosa with you to your new home? Think again, my child. I cannot live *one day* without this boy.'

Months and years followed, during which Mpho considered marriage to Jabu and discussed the matter of her son endlessly with her mother. Making a decision became very complicated. Whenever Mpho found herself persuaded by her mother's arguments, she would suddenly hear unsettling remarks from her sister-in-law concerning Mosa's stay with the family. It became clear that her sister-in-law did not share her mother's view of the matter. And so Mpho swayed in her mind, this way and that, not knowing what to do for the best for all concerned. It was a terrible predicament for her.

On one particular morning, Mpho was about to leave for her work as a domestic employee at the home of the farmer on whose land they lived. Without making a formal request, her sister-in-law remarked casually, 'I hope you will bring mealie tonight as we have no money to replenish it.' Mpho received the message loud and clear – her sister-in-law was saying indirectly, 'Pay for the upkeep of your son.'

At that point, Mpho rescinded the decision she had made when she last spoke to her mother about her son. She knew deep down that she could not leave Mosa behind when she got married. Finally, she went to her mother and told her that she could not follow her advice in this matter. She mentioned in passing the pressures which prevented her from leaving the boy – although she did her best to choose words which would not antagonise her mother against her sister-in-law.

Finding herself in a very difficult position, and anxious to sort things out before Mpho got married, Mpho's mother summoned an inner family circle meeting to discuss the whole question of Mosa's future. She was very upset by what was going on between her daughter and her daughter-in-law.

After intense discussion among the members of the family, with Mpho and her sister-in-law both present, there was unanimous agreement on the matter. Mosa belonged to his mother for as long as she was still a member of her family by domicile. Once she was married with a home of her own, custom and tradition ruled that she must go without Mosa, unless he had been included in the early negotiations over the marriage carried out by the two families. Mpho's family made it very clear to their daughter-in-law that, according to custom, Mosa was a member of his maternal uncle's family.

These decisions were made amid the cries and tears of Mosa's mother, whose grief was aggravated by her sister-in-law's cold and arrogant reaction. But, as was still the practice in the country in the 1960s, Mpho had no choice but to accept the decision of her elders. Accordingly, she swallowed the bitter pill, married the man of her choice and left her son behind with her family.

After a couple of months, the couple left for the big city of Goudveld. There they were exposed to the acute lack of accommodation in the black residential areas. Like many people doing manual labour, their first home was in the backyard of the fine home of their employer. The influx-control regulations were in force so it took some time before they finally qualified as legitimate residents of the urban area. That qualification earned them the right to enter the long, long waiting list of those applying for a house in those 'sacred' urban areas regarded as exclusively 'white people's domain'. Finally, they were lucky enough to get a house they could call home.

It was in that house that the family grew, blessed with both sons and daughters. These new arrivals still left a place for Mosa as part of the family. He visited his mother from time to time and got to know the neighbourhood in which the family lived. His half brothers and sisters accepted him as one of them during his visits, while he was still in school and later when he had started to work. He often went back to his maternal uncle's place after his holiday in the big city feeling happy after being in an atmosphere which accepted him as one of the family. His stepfather received him as one of his own children, a fact which meant much to Mosa's mother.

Mosa grew up to be an industrious and good-looking young man. He found a job in a small town near the farm where his uncle lived. Often driven out by the unpleasant attitude of his uncle's wife, Mosa took refuge in the warmth he received from his first girlfriend's family. They were caring and understanding people.

The strained atmosphere at his uncle's home had forced Mosa at an early age to entertain the thought of getting married and setting up his own home. Time and again, he had pined for his mother's love; and that longing had grown stronger after his grandmother's death. For a long time after she died, he had leaned towards his uncle, who loved and cared for him. But quite often he had sensed some rivalry between himself and his uncle's wife, as if they were in competition for his uncle's attention. That feeling left Mosa very uncomfortable. All he wished was peace and joy in the home. He felt that his aunt did not recognise – far less appreciate – his contributions to the household, big or small.

So, left to himself and away from his mother, Mosa decided that the remedy for his unhappiness and miserable life was to get married. At the beginning, this did indeed seem to be the best solution. After seeking his mother's consent, he married his first love, Dineo, a young woman who worked in the home of the local station manager – an enviable job in the eyes of the young girls of the neighbourhood.

Dineo was admired for her neatness of dress. At work in the kitchen, she would wear a spotless white overall with matching headgear. Off-duty, she dressed in a way that seemed very special to others in her age group. Some of her clothes no doubt came from 'rejects' of her employer's family – that was a common way to replace or augment the wages of employees. But in Dineo's community, which was influenced by conservative rural attitudes, she was seen as a particularly elegant young woman.

From the time of their courtship right up to the first twelve or eighteen months after their marriage, Mosa and Dineo were the talk of the village and the small gossip of the country town. Their marriage was not a formal one. There had been no ceremony approved by the state; nor had they followed the procedures involved in a marriage by custom. But even so, in the village they were seen as the ideal couple. In the town they were seen as '*swart witmense* (black whitepeople)'. Whites saw them as aping whites. From the 1920s up until the 1950s, whites were very threatened by blacks who spoke faultless English. They gave them names like '*swart Engelsman* (black Englishman)'.

When, after two years, the marriage remained childless, attitudes changed towards them – and particularly towards Dineo. To this day, there is a tendency in the black community to blame the wife when there are no children in the marriage. The couple missed the warm greetings that they had been used to from the other young people, along with the warm remarks from elders of the community like '*ngoetsi ea rona* (our daughter-in-law)'.

As time went on and still no children arrived, Mosa and Dineo made the best of their marriage amid criticism, gossip and unfounded allegations. At the same time, Mosa cut down his visits to his mother in Goudveld; his family and work commitments left him with less time for such activities. He kept in touch, though, through correspondence, with his mother and his half brothers and sisters. During one of his visits to Goudveld, his mother found the opportunity to give him guidance and support about relationships with his new family, the continuing problems with his uncle's family and the change of attitude towards himself and Dineo among their neighbours.

One day, when he was working as usual at the railway station of Nukastel, Mosa was in danger of being late back after his lunch break. To gain a few minutes, he started to dash across the railway line. He had not noticed that there was a shunting goods train not far away. Before he realised what was happening, Mosa was hit by that shunting loco-motive; and it crushed both his legs, just below the knees.

He was immediately removed to the local hospital and placed in a section reserved for black patients – a part of the hospital very ill-equipped in every way. Like all the other patients from his community, Mosa accepted the poor level of treatment as normal for black people in South Africa. It was in that hospital that Mosa's legs were amputated up to the knee. He was within hearing distance when some staff and patients uttered strong criticism of his behaviour leading up to the accident. He should have checked to see that nothing was coming before he tried to cross the line, they said. Mosa did his best to ignore what was said, kept cool and carried his cross with much regret and pain.

Like a devoted, loving wife, Dineo visited her husband regularly at the hospital and gave the impression of deep and sympathetic caring. But no one from his city family came to see him. Mosa was concerned about this, but when he asked his wife and other relatives, they assured him that his city family had been informed of his terrible accident. Mosa was very puzzled indeed by the silence from that part of his family. Finally, he resolved to think of all such challenges as fate. This was the only way to cope with what was happening to him.

As time passed by, Dineo's hospital visits became less frequent. When she did come, she gave her husband various reasons for her less regular attendance. Finally, she stopped coming at all. His uncle's family did not come to the hospital either. To Mosa's great concern, their visits had stopped within the first two weeks of his hospitalisation.

Gradually, Mosa adjusted himself to the fact that nobody visited him. With sadness, he came to the conclusion that his wife had probably re-married. She was free to do so, since their marriage was not a formal one and they had no children. But he also became convinced that his city family had never been told of his injury. He lived a very lonely life at the hospital and shared his feelings with no one.

After about nine months in hospital, he began to notice a change for the better. That gave him the hope and courage to forge ahead and think of a future with a brighter outlook. For him the day he was given a wheelchair marked the beginning of new possibilities.

After a time, he started to have more to do with his fellow patients. Together, during the long months of their rehabilitation, they speculated about the future. In these talks, the other patients would discuss what it would be like to see their loved ones back at home. Mosa was uncomfortably aware that, unlike the others, he had had no visitors for a very long time. Even so, he did not lose all hope. The company of his fellow patients helped to give him the courage to accept his condition. As they all got used to managing their wheelchairs, they found themselves able to go wherever they wished within the hospital boundaries; and this gave them a sense of self-confidence and independence.

Eventually, the day arrived for Mosa's discharge from hospital. He had been there for nearly three years. Who would he find when he went back to his uncle's home, the only place he felt he could go? What were his expectations and fears? Only he can say. Certainly, he must have gone through a great deal of mental torture, wondering why no member of the family had visited him for so long. Finally, he settled himself to face the unknown with an open mind.

The police van arrived early to drive him home. Once Mosa was settled inside, the van set out, the driver following the directions which Mosa gave confidently, despite the long time since he had travelled along that road. They arrived at the village and Mosa soon saw some familiar houses. To his amazement, however, his uncle's house was no longer there.

There was nothing – not even the remains of foundations – to confirm that a house had ever stood there.

All efforts to trace where his family had gone were unrewarded. In the end, since the police officers were getting impatient, Mosa had to give them the address of his mother's house in Goudveld, some 400 miles away. As he told the officers where his mother lived, Mosa had no hope at all that they would drive him that long distance. But one of the officers responded to his doubts by saying, 'Do we appear like liars? Don't you trust us, young man?' Regretting that he had expressed any doubt, Mosa just mumbled. 'I did not think you would find it possible to travel so far.' The officer replied, 'This is our job. We know how best to carry it out. You just sit there until we tell you "Get down".' These words sealed Mosa's mouth for the rest of the journey.

Many thoughts passed through Mosa's mind during the long journey that followed. Principal among these was the thought, 'I hope I will find my mother's house still there.' He knew that it was most likely that his uncle's family had left their home only because of a government forced removal. If they had gone of their own will and wish, there would have been old neighbours there who could have told of the move. But no one familiar to Mosa had come to see what was going on after the arrival of the police van. And Mosa was well aware that different households do not usually move away at the same time unless they are forced to do so. He knew, too, that if the family had been forcibly moved, the chances were that they had been moved far away from the hospital where Mosa had spent so much time. And that would have meant great difficulty and expense as far as hospital visits were concerned.

About five hours later, the police van stopped in front of Mosa's second home. The officers came round to the back of the van and helped Mosa out into his wheelchair. By this time, the neighbours were gathering round the gate, asking rhetorical questions like, 'Who can this be?', 'Where is he from?', 'Why is he brought by the police?' Somebody was heard suggesting casually, 'He could be someone just come from serving a long prison term.' The crowd reacted to this remark with reprimands – '*Ag, sis* shut up.' 'You drunk, stop it,' and, 'Stop replying to things you don't know much about.' Under this barrage, the loose-tongued man quickly disappeared from the scene.

Once they realised who Mosa was, the neighbours helped to push the wheelchair into the house. Some were in tears, and many were visibly upset. The older half brothers and sisters recognised Mosa; the younger ones did not know him. All stood there lost for words. It turned out that nobody had had any word of Mosa's accident. As the neighbours and sisters and brothers stood around in dismay, Mosa's eyes moved from corner to corner, and from room to room, looking for something they could not find.

More people, family and neighbours, came into the house. When everybody was seated and there was calm, someone started a hymn, as is the custom when the community is faced with some challenge or disaster. The hymn was followed by a prayer which welcomed Mosa and also prepared him for what was to come. The room was filled with the sounds of soft sobbing and weeping.

When the prayer was over, the closest friend of the family welcomed Mosa and, with great caution, announced to him the death of his mother and his stepfather. That opened a wound which brought pain and sorrow to all those present in that home. The tears which rolled down Mosa's cheeks invited more tears from everyone there. It had been a year, it seemed, since Mpho and Jabu had died.

The eldest half brother was soon contacted and informed of Mosa's arrival. This half brother lived with his family in another part of the township. Despite these commitments, he was doing his best to assume his father's role in a home where there were only youngsters – and where all were unemployed, apart from one of the girls. And she already had several children to support. This eldest half brother pledged to do all that he could to give support to his brother, Mosa. Mpho had achieved much by treating her children as one family.

The reward of waiting

At the turn of the century, polygamy was the accepted norm in some tribal communities in South Africa. It was a common occurrence to find wives of one man very friendly with each other, to the point of wearing similar garments in colour and style. To an outsider, such relationships often seemed unreal and full of pretence; but they were real enough, and were the source of much satisfaction and joy, to the man and women themselves.

Of course, some households were happier than others. A great deal depended on the ability of the husband to maintain peace and order within his family. There was always the danger of petty jealousies and subtle envy spreading among the wives and children.

Khotso was one husband who tried to create the conditions for a harmonious household. He was in his late forties and had one wife. They had two lovely daughters, aged fourteen and ten. For some time, the couple had tried in vain to conceive another child, hoping for a son. Their failure to do so weighed heavily on them both, but especially so on Khotso, who felt his chances of ever having a son were slipping away. In those years, failure to have a son was regarded as a serious setback, since tradition laid it down that sons were the legitimate heirs to the estate of their parents. His wife, Mosidi, also longed for another child but she would have been equally delighted with a girl or a boy.

After much thought and deliberation, Khotso approached his wife and asked her to think seriously about what they should do in order to have a son in the family. The thought of her husband finding a second wife, young enough to bear children, immediately crossed Mosidi's mind. She wondered if that was what her husband meant, and went on to weigh up the implications of such an event. Without making any positive suggestion, Khotso put the problem to his wife several times. His persistence in the matter confirmed her feeling that her husband was indeed entertaining the idea of a second wife. She decided that if he referred to the matter again, she would have a direct reply for him.

It did not take Khotso long to return to the subject; it had clearly become a burning issue for him. Calmly, Mosidi turned to her husband and said, 'Have you ever thought of finding a younger wife who could give birth to your son?' Taken aback by this blunt question, Khotso stumbled over his response. Meanwhile, Mosidi looked straight into his eyes and awaited his reply. It came eventually: 'You – *you* mean I should find another wife? How will you manage in that situation?' Still very cool and calm, Mosidi replied, 'If you do not find another wife, how else do you hope to get a son, seeing that I am no longer able to conceive?' Still bewildered by his wife's forthright manner, Khotso hung down his head, as if in shame, and said, 'Mosidi, please give me time to consider your suggestion. I will return to you with my reply.' Mosidi responded, 'When you do, please also let me know what alternative you had in mind.' In a daze, Khotso left the house and, in a pensive mood, sat under a tree.

That night, as they sat chatting after the evening meal, Khotso returned to the subject – much sooner than his wife had anticipated '*Mma Lerato* (Lerato's mother),' he said, 'I have given our talk very serious thought. To be honest, I never had any alternative thought. I entertained the same idea of finding a second wife. My problem is finding someone to take into the family who will bring blessings and peace, because I never contemplated having any wife other than you.'

This statement came to Mosidi as a revelation. She suddenly felt very guilty, realising that she had suspected that her husband had always wanted a second wife. She had also suspected that he already had someone in mind. She could not look Khotso directly in the eye; instead she looked down, trying to find an answer to her husband's unexpected words. She finally managed these words: 'Thank you for sharing your thoughts so openly, Khotso. I hope you will find guidance in your search for the right woman.' Khotso replied, 'You must be aware, Mosidi, that this is not a task I can undertake without your support and co-operation. The best junior wives are those selected by their senior counterparts. If ever I take a second wife, Mosidi, she will be your choice.'

Khotso was expressing what was common practice in traditional communities in those days. Husbands did indeed rely on their senior wives to recommend someone they felt would be suitable for their husbands and families.

Mosidi felt the weight of the responsibility descend on her. It was a problem she had never dreamt that she would have to address. But she knew that it was imperative for their family to have a son: the peace and harmony of the household depended on it. Recently, she had seen Khotso drifting into a tense, solemn mood; and she found it increasingly difficult to cheer him up, a task which previously she had always carried out easily and with joy. She decided that she would have to consider her husband's wish with seriousness and urgency.

Mosidi's relaxed nature and respect for people had earned her many friends among the community's women, young and old. She knew several homes in which there lived respectable young women – one of whom might make a suitable junior wife for Khotso. Any decision of this type, Mosidi knew, was a risky one; and she gave herself ample time to look for the right woman. Meanwhile, Khotso kept his

thoughts, fears and expectations to himself and asked no
questions about this sensitive and important subject.

After a month or two – a period which to Khotso seemed
like a decade – Mosidi reopened the difficult subject. She
chose a time late at night when they had already gone to bed.
'Khotso,' she began, 'you know I have never rested since
you expressed your fervent desire to have a son. Because I
have accepted the Christian faith, I have found it very difficult
to accept that we should introduce polygamy into our home.
All the same, having said that, I want you to know that I
have been very vigilant in looking for a mature young
woman who would fit into our home, whom you would
love and cherish at all times, and who, I would hope, would
have love and respect for our family.' Mosidi's voice became
shaky and soft as she uttered her final sentence: 'She comes
from a good home, if that should mean anything.'

The only words that managed to leave Khotso's lips were,
'Thank you, Mosidi. You will tell me the rest tomorrow.'
Khotso was a Christian worshipper in name only; but he
understood the importance of the Church to his wife. Mosidi
was pleased and surprised that her husband asked no more
at this point. The candle light was put out and they soon fell
asleep.

After about two days of tense silence, Khotso resumed the
talk, saying, 'Mosidi, I am now ready to hear your full report
of the woman you have found to be your helper in this
home.' Khotso was overwhelmed by what Mosidi had to tell
him. She had selected Fumane, daughter of the right-hand
man of the Chief of Bafokeng village. She was a good-
looking woman in her middle twenties, well-groomed and
from a good background and home. She was known in the
community as an industrious, diligent woman – qualities
highly prized in wives-to-be.

Khotso and Mosidi were not wealthy. They worked hard
for what they owned; and they were respected in their community. It was counted an honour, then, for Fumane's family

to be brought together with Khotso's family in this way. In a short time, all the negotiations were completed and Fumane proudly joined Khotso's family as his second wife. Because of her youth, Fumane was very confident that she would soon be mother to Khotso's only son.

At the beginning, everything seemed to go according to plan. There appeared to be a healthy relationship between Mosidi and Fumane. Fumane was indeed an asset to the family in terms of her contribution to the household chores. She was also a warm, pleasant young woman who soon took to Khotso's children. In their turn, they responded to her with love. Before too long, Khotso's family became the envy of the village because of the easy harmony prevailing there.

From month to month, Fumane's family anxiously monitored her appearance, trying to judge whether she was yet expectant. But months passed by without any sign of such a condition. And then, to everybody's shock, some six months after Fumane's arrival in the family, it came to light that Mosidi herself was expectant. Her youngest girl at that time was ten years of age. This discovery started a series of conflicts within the family.

Within two months of the confirmation of Mosidi's pregnancy, Fumane began to show signs of depression and withdrawal. She took less and less part in household work – an area in which she had previously excelled. She spoke less, too, keeping to herself most of the time. Khotso and Mosidi guessed that she was overcome by self-pity on account of her failure to conceive before Mosidi, who was by far her senior in years. But all their efforts to make her feel better failed. These developments clearly embarrassed her family. Gradually, the atmosphere in the home, which had earlier been the envy of the village, turned sour.

Mosidi tried to support Fumane by looking to her for help in all ways when her pregnancy advanced and became a burden to her. She hoped in this way to win Fumane round, to bring them closer together and to reduce Fumane's tension, anxiety and insecurity. But Fumane closed up, sharing her problems and concerns with nobody in her new home – not even with Khotso. She ended up by distancing herself from all members of the family.

In those early years, when black people lived from the land, custom demanded that after confinement the new mother remained in the house for a period of three months. During that time, she had people around her who were assigned the special duties of nursing her, cooking for her, carrying out all the normal household tasks, and helping her with the baby. Under normal circumstances Fumane, as Khotso's second wife, would have been responsible for allocating duties to those who came to assist in the house at the time when Mosidi was due for confinement. But her sudden change of attitude made it difficult for people in the home to communicate and plan with her.

Fumane's state of mind also affected her relationship with her husband. Khotso began to show signs of embarrassment and guilt; also perhaps of regret over his decision to take a second wife, since Mosidi's baby might well be a boy. All in all, his life was not a comfortable one at this time, though he awaited the birth of his baby with great excitement. Fumane's difficult manner had brought Khotso and Mosidi closer together. Meanwhile, much against Khotso's will, Fumane became a constant visitor to her parents' home.

The arrival of the new baby – a son – was the greatest day in the life of Khotso's family. But it seemed to spell doom for Fumane. The baby, who resembled his father and was Khotso's great pride and joy, seemed to cement the parents' relationship still further. But Fumane appeared to be even more strained and tense and took to going to her parents even more frequently. Sometimes she spent the night at their home. Khotso's family tried to understand her problem and to accommodate her to the best of their ability. They took it that she was suffering from the pain of failing to conceive while Mosidi, a much older woman, had given birth to the first son in the family. They did their best to show her that they felt for her; but Fumane did not respond to their support.

The baby was about two months old when Fumane left for her parents' home without telling her husband that she was leaving. When she had stayed away for the unusually long period of three or four days, Khotso discussed the matter with Mosidi and then went after Fumane to find out what had happened to her. Before leaving, he checked the room which he shared with Fumane – and found that she had removed all that belonged to her. This came as a shock to Khotso; and he refrained from sharing the discovery with Mosidi through fear of unsettling her.

At Fumane's parents' house, Khotso was dismayed to learn that their daughter had reported that she had suffered emotional torture and humiliation in her new home. And because of that, she had pleaded with them not to intervene in any way. Finally, she had left her parents' home to go to the city to find a job and, she hoped, to forget the traumatic experience she had gone through. It has to be remembered that, in those years, failure to conceive was seen as a general indictment of a woman's behaviour and character.

Fumane's abrupt and unhappy departure made a deep impression on Khotso. He was convinced that the events of the previous months held a message for him. He began to see his wife in a fresh light, putting a new value on her calm nature, her confidence in herself and in others, and her respect for other people. In his mind, he relived the time when Fumane was part of their family; and he thought of the difficulties created by Fumane's attitude. Once again, he was filled with admiration and respect for the way in which Mosidi had responded to Fumane's whims and moods.

Their baby was about a year old when Khotso unfolded himself to his wife. '*Mma Lerato*,' he started, 'all through our married life of sixteen years, I have never doubted your integrity, dependability, good judgment, unselfishness at all times, and your honesty and sincerity when making decisions. I have always been fully aware of these rare qualities and attributes of yours. Today I am openly acknowledging them to you. I thank you for who you are. I thank my God and my ancestors for giving me a wife with such rare gifts of understanding and accepting, sometimes at your own expense, other people's shortcomings and abilities, failures and successes, likes and dislikes. This acknowledgment of who you are has increased my faith in my Creator and persuaded me that I alone do not have the power to direct my destiny. I thank you for all that. I thank all the powers which gave us this son.' Here, Khotso cuddled the baby, Mpho ('Gift'). 'He is fully the brother of Lerato ('Love') and Basetsana ('Girl'). For this I am grateful.'

Mosidi had been listening with concentration to what her husband said. Once Khotso had finished his long, cathartic speech, she took some time to respond to him. Then, in her usual calm manner, she turned to him, saying, 'Thank you, *Rra Lerato* (Lerato's father), for all the kind things you have said to me about me. For me, the greatest message that has come out of this experience has been the affirmation of the love, support and guidance of our Creator. My faith is anchored in these realities. Time and again, I have shared with you my commitment to worship and my dedication to my faith. Somehow I was convinced that our prayers and pleas for a son would be rewarded. At the time, however, I found it very difficult to communicate that to you. My trust has not been in vain. My hopes have been fulfilled.'

In complete surrender, Khotso handed over everything, saying, 'From today, your faith will be my faith, your God my God, your hopes my hopes, your trust my trust. You have been the pillar, strength, support and guide of this family. Let it always be so.'

Within six months, Khotso was dead. Those words of his remained a mainstay in Mosidi's life. In her grief, she was much comforted by the fact that her husband died a convert and a devoted worshipper.

The strongest link in a chain is its weakest point

Pulane was born into a poor farming community near the small country town of Tanu. Almost every shop in that town traded in food, household utensils and farming implements. Pulane went up to standard six at school, the highest class that could be attained then by able black pupils in that area. There was no doubt that Pulane was an intelligent pupil; but there was no opportunity for her to progress with her education and achieve some kind of professional qualification in the rural town of Tanu in the 1960s.

When she left school, the poverty of her family meant that she was compelled to take any employment that could earn her a living. So, for about a year, she worked as a farm labourer. Then she found work in cafés and restaurants which served the travellers passing through the country town. She was never idle, always willing to work even if the job was far below her capabilities. Many people admired her, parents in the community and employers alike. Many parents of young men saw in this industrious young woman the ideal prospective daughter-in-law. Diligence and industriousness were perhaps the qualities most highly prized in the black community by parents looking out for a wife for their sons.

As fate would have it, Pulane fell in love with a young man from the far-off country of Boshothu. Mmuso was also an industrious, respectable person. Soon the couple got married; and the early years of their married life were very happy ones. Mmuso was a good husband, taking a great interest in all matters to do with his family. Within eighteen months, the couple were blessed with a baby boy named Lefa ('Wealth'). Like all young parents, Pulane and Mmuso showered their son with love and tender care. Whenever they could afford to, they brought home lovely presents for the baby.

Like Pulane, Mmuso never turned down a job because it lacked prestige. And when a job came up in one of the big cities, the family moved there. Maboneng ('Lights') was some fifty times bigger than Tanu. All the streets in Maboneng were well-tarred and fully lit. Every quarter of an hour, trains carried commuters in and out of the city. Pulane and Mmuso were amazed by their new environment, so full of activity and movement. It was with joy and pride that Mmuso joined the movement of the numerous labourers who travelled to and from work in the city every day.

They lived first with Pulane's family in Sewetsong, a township about twenty-five kilometres from Maboneng. Many families in the township were homeless. Some of them lived in discarded cars or in very dilapidated shacks made of cardboard and sacks; others roamed the streets, without shelter from rain, cold, heat or darkness. That era was the forerunner of 'homelessness', now at its peak in the black community.

The city itself was inhabited exclusively by white people, apart from the black people who were employed as domestic workers. Many mothers regarded their employment as a godsend because it gave them earnings and shelter. But there was great pain in the fact that their employers did not allow their husbands to live with them and that the laws of the country forbade even their young children to be with them. Husbands and children were regarded as 'illegal' residents and, if they were found on the employer's premises, they were often harassed by police, who would remove them forcibly from the premises and sometimes send them to prison.

Against this background, Mmuso and Pulane were very fortunate to have a home with Pulane's family. Like all township dwellers, Mmuso left home at about 7.00 a.m. in order to be in time for work at 8.30 a.m. Public transport was a real problem in this community as it was always crowded, scarce and erratic in arrival and departure times. But since it was common practice in industry to cut the wages of latecomers, workers by and large took great pains to be on time for work and thus protect their meagre earnings.

By the time they arrived in the township, Pulane and Mmuso had another baby – a boy again, who was given the name of Mpho ('Gift'). This new arrival added to the joy of the family. Even with this added responsibility, Pulane still managed her household duties efficiently and kept her husband's clothes neat and trim. Since Mmuso was able and willing to provide for his family, Pulane stayed at home to care for the family. Being the industrious woman she was, she also contributed greatly to the running of her uncle's family. All in all, the domestic situation was a happy one.

The family had been established in Maboneng for three years when a third child – a girl – was born. She was named Lerato ('Love'). While the parents were very happy with the new arrival, they soon realised that the meagre wage on which they were living could no longer meet their needs. To alleviate the extra economic burden brought about by the growth of the family, Pulane started to toy with the idea of finding a job. Hesitant at first, she decided she had to look for the right time in which to broach the subject with her husband.

One particular day, Mmuso returned from work, as usual, at about 6.45 p.m. He turned to his wife, saying, '*Dumela Mma* (Good afternoon, mother).' (Used in a situation like this, 'mother' means 'mother of my children'.) Pulane replied, '*Dumela Rra* (Good afternoon, father),' and immediately gave her husband water with which to wash his hands before taking tea. Then followed talk about the happenings of the day, broken by a question here and laughter there. All this time, Pulane was preparing the evening meal.

In the breaks in their conversation, Mmuso took time to chat with his sons. The boys told him about the happenings of their day – in particular, about how some older boys had bullied them. Mmuso listened to them with interest and care, knowing that they looked to him for guidance on how to behave. In a kindly way, he advised them, '*Le itoanele banna* (Fend for yourselves, chaps).' Any on-looker would have noticed the love, intimacy, caring and friendship between that father and his sons.

After saying grace, the family sat down to their meal. It was clear that they enjoyed their humble, simple supper; that the father was proud of providing for his family; and that the mother acknowledged and appreciated her husband's efforts and achievements.

It was after supper, when all the children had gone to bed and the couple were having tea and chatting, that Pulane raised the subject of her looking for a job. Being anxious not to make her husband feel guilty, she approached the matter in a slightly roundabout way: '*Rragwe Lefa* (Lefa's father),' she began, using an affectionate form of address, 'I wonder if, like me, you have been feeling the financial strain in the family during recent months?' Mmuso replied, 'Pulane, it is not surprising that you have been feeling the strain. After all, you are the one who runs the house and you are always trying to make ends meet. Remember too that the family has grown.'

Pulane welcomed this very understanding response. She felt deep down that now was the right moment to approach her husband, about the possibility of her looking for a job. She continued: 'I have been thinking that, before too long, Lerato will be old enough to start at the crèche and that would give me an opportunity to seek work. What do you think?' Mmuso replied, '*Mma Lerato*, she will need you for the next six to nine months before you can leave her at the crèche.' Pulane accepted this, and stressed that this was the time-scale in her mind. They agreed, then, on what should happen; and Mmuso made the comment that the timing would be good since Pulane's search for work would coincide with the ending of the year.

In due course, the end of the year came, and Pulane found a temporary job in domestic service, filling in for a friend who had gone on holiday. By this time, Lefa was eight years old, Mpho was six, and the baby, Lerato, was eighteen months.

It was accepted practice for casual workers, like Mmuso, to come home late on Fridays since they did some shopping after knocking off from work and receiving their wages. They generally arrived home an hour or an hour and a half later than the usual time.

On one particular Friday in December, however, Pulane started to get worried when Mmuso was still not home by 9 p.m. This had never happened before; and Christmas time, Pulane knew, was often marked by misfortunes and unsettling tragedies. Her uneasy thoughts conjured up a whole variety of different situations. Was he badly injured and in hospital? Was he murdered? Was he arrested? Had they had a closing party at work? (But he had not mentioned any party.) Even if there had been a party, Mmuso did not take liquor, so he could not be lying somewhere drunk.

And in among these worries was another, terrible, uncertainty. Where was her son, Mpho? That morning, Mmuso had requested his wife that their younger son should accompany him to town. He had never asked this before and, although a little puzzled by the request, Pulane had agreed to the arrangement. And now both father and son were missing. Pulane turned her thoughts over endlessly, in silence. 'Where can they be?' she asked herself. 'What can have become of them?' She refrained from raising any alarm in the neighbourhood. She told herself that the best thing was to wait in case they were delayed somewhere.

Eventually, Pulane, Lefa and Lerato ate their evening meal together – a meal which they did not enjoy. Naturally, the children soon showed signs of fatigue and fell asleep. Pulane then put them to bed. The silence that followed ate into her and haunted her. The slightest sound made her jump to her feet and rush to the window. Footsteps, coughs, laughter, conversation, passing cars – all drew her to the window and sent her back unrewarded. In between times, she lay next to her baby, hoping to fall asleep – but all in vain. From time to time, she told herself that Mmuso had gone to visit friends; but a voice inside her whispered that the fact that he had taken the child made this impossible.

Finally, in the early hours of the morning, Pulane managed to fall asleep. When she opened her eyes, the room was flooded with bright light. Her mind, however, was still clouded, full of dark thoughts and imaginings. She could not think straight; her head was heavy with sleep and fatigue and her heart was beating heavily. She looked round the house, hoping that Mmuso had come in while she was asleep. He was not there. Suddenly, she heard herself ask, 'Mmuso, where have you gone with my son?' The echo of her voice in the room awakened no response.

Once her uncle's family were up, Pulane joined them and shared with them her fears and concern about her husband and son. They were hurt that she had not woken them the night before so that they could share her plight. After some deliberation, they decided to report the matter to the police. Pulane's uncle accompanied her to make the report. Three hours later, they returned home, Pulane dragging her feet, weeping, and in complete disarray.

On her return, she considered going to Mmuso's place of work, but soon remembered that they did not work on Saturdays. The weekend dragged by endlessly for Pulane and her family. Lefa, the oldest child, kept on asking his mother when his father would return with Mpho. This added to Pulane's burden of worry; but nothing she said could stop the boy from asking his question and getting into a state of panic. Every knock on the door brought new hope of news of her husband's plight. But no news came.

As Pulane sat pondering over her problem, she could not help but count herself lucky that, for the past three weeks, she had been working in a job. She could not imagine what her present situation would be like if she had not been earning some money.

On the Monday, she reported her plight to her employers and was given leave to go to her husband's place of employment in order to trace his movements on the Friday. She went there hoping against hope to find some clues as to what might have happened. Her own conviction was that her husband and son must have met their misfortune on their way home after leaving the office.

As she approached Mmuso's place of employment, she began to get cold feet and was afraid to go inside. 'What if they say they last saw him when he left for home?' she asked herself. 'What will I do then?' After spending some time debating with herself whether or not to enter the office, she finally summoned up courage and walked in. Almost immediately, she met someone she knew was a colleague of her husband, since Mmuso had once taken him home. She looked into the man's face, trying to find some clues there. But his expression was perfectly normal; if anything, he seemed surprised to see her. Trying to keep calm, Pulane greeted him. He returned the greeting and then asked, quite casually, '*Molato keng Pulane? O batlong mo ka nako e?* (Is there anything wrong, Pulane? What brings you here so early?)' The tone of his voice told Pulane at once that he knew nothing of the problem which had brought her to the office. All the same, she forged ahead and said, 'I have come to see my husband. Can you find him for me, please?'

Pulane read doubt, hesitation and confusion in the man's face as he asked, 'You mean you want to talk to Mmuso?' Taking advantage of his confusion, she responded, 'Yes.

Why, where is he?' Puzzled by Pulane's questions, the man offered her a seat and persuaded her to wait for a short time. Meanwhile, he went into an office – to call Mmuso, Pulane hoped. At that point, she did not know what to think or expect. She was convinced that her husband had met with some serious accident. 'My son,' she whispered to herself. She struggled hard to stop tears running from her eyes.

Mmuso's friend returned and gently took a seat next to Pulane. As she looked into his face, she could see that his whole attitude had changed. He positioned himself in a way that unsettled and frightened her. He then looked straight into her face as he said to her, 'Pulane, I am really amazed that you are here to see your husband. What did he say to you when he left home on Friday?' 'Nothing unusual,' she replied. 'I find this very strange and so does the rest of the office,' he answered. 'Because, as far as we know, your husband left the office at about eleven o'clock in the morning after collecting his wages. He was intending to do some shopping in town, along with his son. He returned here after four o'clock in the afternoon, bade us all farewell and told us that he was going home to Boshothu for his Christmas holiday with his son. He had long ago arranged with the office to leave on Friday. You mean you knew nothing about this arrangement? He did not tell you anything about it?' These words and questions flowed out of his mouth, with no pause for thought. He seemed to be in a daze. But Pulane was much more dazed and numbed by what she heard.

Her baby strapped to her back and her arms folded, Pulane stood up. She stared fixedly at the ground without saying a word for the better part of ten minutes. Then, as if seeking the strength to talk, she slowly raised her head, looking at Mmuso's friend. Speaking to him – but yet not speaking to him – she said, 'Why does Mmuso do this to me? We had no quarrel when he left for work on Friday. Why does he treat me like this?' and then, as if coming out of a trance, she said to her husband's colleague, 'Pitso, thank you for everything. I have no reason to doubt all that you have told me, even though I find it difficult to find any reason for Mmuso's actions. Thank you.' Pitso replied, 'Pulane, wait – don't you want to talk to someone senior here?' 'Are they going to tell me any more than you have just told me?' Pulane asked. 'No, not really,' replied Pitso. Without any further comment, Pulane said goodbye and departed, leaving Pitso sitting glued to the bench. As she turned the corner, she looked back. He was still sitting there, cupping his face in his hands.

Without wasting any time, Pulane visited all the offices she needed to in order to arrange a journey to Boshothu. Her purpose was to find her son and bring him back to Maboneng. Once she reached Boshothu, she faced many bureaucratic procedures. But, after she had put her case to the authorities there, they found Mmuso and ordered him to produce Mpho. Without delay, he did so. Pulane took Mpho back home with her the next day.

The seemingly strong chain of this marriage, then, had snapped at its weakest point. The cultural differences between the two had made it impossible for them to communicate on anything other than a superficial level.

Pulane's fine qualities emerged strongly after this traumatic experience. She firmly pulled herself together and found a steady, rewarding job as a domestic worker. She also looked after her uncle who was now ailing.

In due course, she herself became the proud owner of the house in which she and her children lived. In the course of her job, she made friends with some of her employers, a few of them from far-off countries over the seas. Her courage, determination, resourcefulness and industriousness carried her through all the pain and difficulty she encountered. Wishing for her children greater opportunities than she had had, she encouraged them in every way to make the most of their education. From her ordeal, she emerged as a model and an inspiration to the younger generation – and, in particular, to young women.

Part Four

How Much Does a Roof Cost?

Almost as soon as it gained power in South Africa in the late 1940s, the Nationalist Party imposed harsh and separate rules on the government of black residential areas. To this day, 'local councils' exist only to segregate blacks from other race groups and to enforce the inhuman regulations which are necessary to do this. Black residents have no say in the running of their local authorities.

One aspect of the injustice which results from this system is the chaos surrounding the issue of home-ownership. From the early 1950s to the mid–1970s, black women were barred from owning their own houses – or from being the tenants of rented houses. Only married men were allowed to own or rent houses. This meant that, when widowed or divorced, black women would automatically lose their homes. Even when a marriage ended because of a husband's cruelty or neglect and even when a wife was given custody of the children, the common home ended up as the legal property of the husband.

Many, many women suffered because of this unjust ruling. But, as the story 'Choosing a hat for a husband' shows, perhaps it was the widows who suffered most. This was because they were confronted with the stark choice: find a new husband or lose your home.

Yes, during this period, the choice was just that. Before the 1976 unrest, it was common practice for widows to be summoned to their local municipal offices. There, they would be warned that, in the interests of themselves and their families, they should re-marry in order to keep their homes. The women might say that they were still in mourning and were bound by tradition not to re-marry before the lapse of a certain period of time. They might say that they were still in deep grief over the death of their husbands. They might say that they had no wish in the world to re-marry. But all in vain. All these reasons would be dismissed by the authorities as worthless.

You can imagine some of the results of this pressure to re-marry. Many widows ended up with husbands they did not want. And, a short time after re-marrying, some widows ended up in the street with their children: having found an even newer love, their spouses had chased them away from the common home. By interfering in people's lives in this way, the authorities exposed many women and children – daughters, in particular – to traumatic abuse. When you realise that the population of Soweto alone is estimated at between one and a half and two million, you can appreciate that scores of thousands of black women suffered from this barbaric practice.

A rumour spread in those years that some widows who were refusing to re-marry were ordered to appear before an official. Once there, they were shown several men's hats – and were then told to pick one of them. The owner of the chosen hat would end up the husband of the woman who had picked it. Needless to say, such marriages usually had disastrous endings. Many women in this situation suffered untold hardships from men who never loved them – men whose interest was primarily to own a house and to use that house for their own purposes. The rightful owners of the house – the mother and her children – all too often ended up homeless and destitute.

And so, for many years, this was the plight of black women in the urban areas of South Africa. Perhaps it was an indirect way of repatriating them to the so-called 'home-lands' – where, of course, they were unknown and where they knew no one.

After the 1976 unrest, there were new attempts to try to address the social, economic and educational problems of the townships. One of the bodies prominent in these attempts was the Urban Foundation, an oganisation formed by the businessmen of South Africa. At first, since it was started by whites and run by whites, the black community saw this organisation as an extension of the government. But when it took a clear stand on home-ownership policy for blacks, the abolition of influx control regulations and the educational system, its image improved for many people in the community. However, to this day the Urban Foundation is still seen as a body which provides jobs for whites – especially those jobs that provided pensions. The ratio of 1:6 blacks to whites in the board of management leaves much to be desired for the blacks who serve on the board.

Many of these issues have still not been finally resolved; but in the early 1980s, black urban residents began to be allowed to buy plots and build homes on a 99-year land tenure lease. The fact that they can now own their houses has contributed to the status of black women and to the overall uplifting of the community, as well as to the security of individual families. Up to the introduction of the 99-year land tenure lease, all houses in the townships were rented from the existing local authority, except for a few which were said to be bought, but their ownership was not clearly defined. Up to that time all houses were 'owned' by the male head of each family.

The second story here, 'Granny Basadi', illustrates the plight of many elderly people in a community where there are far too few houses for far too many people.

From the 1950s to the late 1970s, the building of houses in the black townships was frozen – no doubt as a way of forcing repatriation to the 'homelands'. This created long waiting-lists for those who applied for homes; and 'waiting' in this case could mean applying for ten to twenty years and still being given no home. The serious problem of homelessness that resulted from this policy was aggravated by the endless 'forced removals', when established neighbourhoods were torn to the ground and the people transported to desolate places which lacked basic services of any kind. Naturally, these people drifted back to the urban areas where they settled, regardless of all restrictive regulations, to find some accommodation in one urban area or another.

This lack of houses has created a situation where many people exploit others for their private gain. There are reports of community councillors who have accepted bribes for houses built by private enterprise. Many families have lost their hard-earned savings in this way – and have still ended up with no home.

And then there is the vulnerability of elderly people. Since wages generally are so meagre for blacks, once people stop working they start their old age almost as beggars. They have never enjoyed any form of insurance and have never found it possible to save money out of their small earnings. This means that, before very long, the rent for their homes becomes a burden – particularly as there is no system of rent rebate for elderly black people in South Africa. Some old people depend entirely on their old age pension, which is paid only at intervals of six weeks and does not amount even to R200 (about £45). These old people have to live hand-to-mouth. Only a very few people are lucky enough to be helped by their children or to benefit from insurance or some legacy from an employer.

Many old people have ended up sharing their rent and home with some other person or couple. A few of these arrangements have worked out well. Many others have ended in difficulty or disaster for the old people involved. Some old people have seen their homes taken from them by those they invited in, and have ended up homeless and destitute.

Others become sub-tenants in their own homes, at the mercy of their 'helpers'.

In some cases, old people have been done out of their homes by some distant cunning relative, who has offered to live with 'dear' aunt, uncle or granny. Sometimes these old people have ended up in a congested 'transit camp' – or, if they are lucky, in an old people's home. Not all old people end their lives in such miserable, unplanned circumstances – but many such stories are told in Soweto every week.

Choosing a hat for a husband

John was born in September 1938 in Troyville, Johannesburg, in the back-yard room of the home of a renowned missionary, Ray Phelps. John's parents both worked in this home.

Ray Phelps and his wife, Dora, came from Illinois in America but had worked long and hard in South Africa, contributing greatly to the improvement of the living standards of black people.

From the beginning, Ray and Dora Phelps took John into their house and nurtured him as their own child. John's mother had complete freedom to care for her child in the wholesome surroundings of the main building. Unlike most employers, the missionary and his wife refused to have the child grow up in the back-yard room; instead, John's parents used this room as their bedroom. They had their meals and spent their relaxation time in the main house with the Phelps family.

John's father, Daniel, was a handyman at the missionary's home and also helped out at the Bantu Men's Social Centre, a place of recreation for blacks and other non-white groups. It was in this centre that Dr Phelps carried out many welfare and recreational programmes for the deprived communities living around Johannesburg. He and his wife also established and ran the first institution in the country to train black social workers – the Jan Hofmeyr School of Social Work.

Daniel was a valuable member of staff at the centre, giving his services gladly. Later in his life, John always had a clear memory of the happy times he spent there with his father and Dr Phelps.

In John's early childhood, when he started to read and write, the missionary would give him simple books to read during the day when he was left alone with his mother. John had firm instructions from Dr Phelps that, when the Phelps family returned at the end of the day, John should be able to give a full account of what he had read. John was told, too, to do his reading properly in the reading room of the house. He used to enjoy these assignments and carried them out fully.

These early, secure years established a firm foundation for John's personal growth, character and health, giving him the strength to face the many challenges that lay ahead of him. Later, he himself said that the Phelps family had nurtured him.

When John was five years old, his parents' desire to have a house of their own was fulfilled when they managed to rent a municipal house in the Orlando township which was established in the early 1930s. Meanwhile, John continued his education under the guardianship of Dr Phelps. At the age of ten, he rejoined his parents in Orlando, having been enrolled by Dr Phelps at the American Board Mission school there. John subsequently obtained his standard six certificate and went on to Adams College in Natal, another progressive school. At the age of twenty, he matriculated successfully from there.

One year later, his father died and the family's world was turned upside-down. Very shortly after Daniel's death, the family was threatened with losing their home. His widow was given the ultimatum of finding a new husband or surrendering the house. When John's mother refused to go along with the practice of 'choosing a hat' – and thus a new husband – the family had to think of some other way of saving their home. It happens that at that time, there was a great shortage of accommodation for single people, and the Council had ruled that housing should be allocated only to married men. So in this desperate situation, the only sure way seemed to be for John, young as he was and as yet with no secure job, to find a wife. Once he was married, he would be allowed to take over the tenancy of the house.

And so, to retain the house that Daniel had left them and to save his mother from the humiliation of a forced marraige, John decided to enter a marriage of convenience. There was hardly any time for preparation, emotional or practical; and there was certainly no opportunity for an enjoyable court-ship.

Even after John got married, the future looked bleak. The family had no savings to fall back on and the only money coming in was what John earned in his employment as a taxi driver. This amounted to only two pounds five shillings a month; and from this John had to pay rent, buy food and meet the other household needs. The only thing the family owned was an old Buick that had belonged to Daniel.

They knew that they could not survive very long in this situation – particularly since John's mother was beginning to suffer from ill health. After thinking long and hard about what they could do to make some more money, John per-suaded his mother that they should trade in the old Buick in order to buy a new second-hand car which they could rank as a taxi of their own. His mother agreed to try out this plan; but she had little hope of it succeeding since they had no money with which to supplement the trade-in value of the old car.

They set out one morning to look for the right car, John's mother trailing along behind him, dressed in her black mourning clothes. They entered a few car sales places with-out finding anything which impressed John. But eventually, John's eyes fell on a car which he fancied for his business. After he made it clear that he was serious about wanting that particular car, he and his mother were invited into the office to finalise the deal. The first question the dealer asked was, 'How much deposit are you able to put down on the car?' John replied steadily and with confidence, 'Nothing on top of the Buick I am trading in.'

Taken aback by John's reply, and with his eyes almost bulging out of his head, the car dealer responded, 'Not on my life can you get this car without paying some deposit in cash.' In a very composed manner, John answered him, 'Sir, you can see that my mother here is a raw widow. Her husband has just died. As the only son in the family, I have to provide for her. I have no job. My last hope is to get this car and run it as a taxi, making a living out of this and also paying you back what I owe you out of my takings.'

When the car dealer heard this, he became furious and turned on John, almost jabbing him in the eye with a finger which was pointing wildly towards the door. 'Young man,' he barked, 'get out of my shop before I call the police to take you and your mother away.' You can imagine what John's mother felt at these words.

Still set on getting his way, John turned to face the dealer, saying, 'Please understand my plea. Trust me. Give me the car. On my honour, I will pay the instalments regularly.' John then squatted firmly in the centre of the floor and announced, 'I am not moving from your shop without the car – even if you do call the police to remove me.' And he said again, 'I repeat that I will pay you regularly. My mother is my witness. She depends on this car' – and here John pointed at the vehicle – 'for her livelihood.'

At this point, the car dealer looked straight into John's eyes and asked him, 'Do you really expect me to trust you when I do not know you?' John replied simply, 'Please do.' There were a few moments of silence, during which the car dealer seemed to be consulting his inner self. Then he turned to John's mother and said, 'I give this car to your son, for your sake. I rely on you for the promise he makes.' 'Thank you,' John said. And he pulled his driver's licence from his pocket with the words, 'My mother, myself and this document will use this car for your benefit and for ours as well.'

With the car in his possession, John took his mother along to obtain the registration of the car as a taxi. He used the same approach with the officials as he had done with the car dealer. He told them calmly and clearly about the death of his father, the absence of a breadwinner in the family, his mother's ill-health and unemployed state and his marriage of convenience. He presented the argument that he had to earn money for all these reasons – and also in order to pay the dealer for the car. All this finally earned him the taxi licence which allowed him to trade.

John kept his promise. From the time he started to trade, he paid the car dealer regularly, at the rate of £100 a month. Within six months, he had paid off the car – to the complete amazement of the dealer. He got his second car with ease from that same man.

John's new business enabled the family to survive. But after a few years, he felt that he was in something of a dead-end. He was very frustrated to find that, with his only qualifications being his matriculation certificate and his driver's licence, it was difficult for him to gain interesting and well-paid work. The harsh and unjust regulations which governed the running of municipal housing had played havoc with the lives of everyone in the family.

John's life experience has haunted him to a point where he has set himself the challenge of helping young black students to use and understand computers and thereby help their future employment prospects.

Granny Basadi

Nkgono (Granny) Basadi lived with her husband, Mr Tusho, in a rented house in the black township of Sarona. They had lived in that same house for many years. Although they had no children of their own, the couple were very close to Mr Tusho's three nephews. From their childhood, these boys had been very attached to their uncle's family. And, after the death of both their parents, they became part of the family in a very real sense. Outsiders thought of these boys as the couple's own children.

Basadi and her husband were both accustomed to working very hard. Mr Tusho had worked in the building trade since his youth in the early 1930s and he was well-versed in most of the skills of that industry. He could lay bricks, undertake carpentry, and carry out plumbing and painting jobs with great confidence and ability. Because he possessed these skills, he was never without employment for any length of time. Basadi herself had worked in a factory since she was a young girl.

Husband and wife were very attached to each other. From quite an early stage in their marriage, they accepted the fact that they would have no children of their own; and, unlike many other young couples in the community, they did not allow this fact to drive them apart. They lived for each other, making the best of what they had – and that was a great deal. Their home was full of warmth and love, the nephews seeming almost like their own children; and they were loved and respected by their families and neighbours.

Sadly, a serious illness struck Mr Tusho. *Nkgono* Basadi kept her job during this time and was helped a great deal by her nephews, who were still young and attending school. When it became clear that her husband's situation was deteriorating by the day, she discussed the family situation with him. They agreed that it would be sensible to invite a couple, relatives of the family, to move in with them and help nurse Mr Tusho during the day while Basadi was at work.

At the same time, one of the nephews, Khumo, worried about his uncle and aunt, decided to live with them so as to be able to run errands when necessary. Khumo lived with the family in the main house; while the couple, along with their daughter, occupied the two outside rooms.

After an extended illness, Mr Tusho died. Basadi was very grateful to have the supportive company of her nephew Khumo, who by this time was at work and was making serious plans to get married. Accepted by all as the son of the family, Khumo was regarded as the legitimate male heir to the estate of his uncle-father so they were able to retain the house. This, together with the fact that she had a couple living with her as sub-tenants, made Basadi less vulnerable to eviction.

When Khumo did get married, he and his wife made their home with his aunt Basadi. Meanwhile, the couple who had been invited to help nurse Mr Tusho continued to live in the two outside rooms. At first, the new household worked very well; indeed, many relatives and neighbours envied what seemed to them to be a rare and special domestic harmony. But with the passing of time, Pelo, Khumo's bride, began to tell her husband about her wish to have a home of their own. All efforts by her husband to dissuade her from wishing to leave fell on deaf ears.

This left Khumo in a very delicate position, particularly as his aunt had no idea that Pelo was discontented in any way. He spent sleepless nights trying to work out how to make his wife happy without making his aunt-mother unhappy. Eventually, he shared his worries with Basadi. She was taken aback by what she heard as she had suspected nothing of the kind. She spoke to Pelo directly about the matter and discovered that Pelo was indeed determined to have a home of her own, even if, in the short term, it meant hiring a room. Being by nature a peaceful and courageous woman, Basadi decided that rather than sacrifice Khumo's marriage and therefore his happiness, she should give them the freedom to do what they deemed best for their family.

Accordingly, with Basadi's permission and support, Khumo and Pelo started looking for a room in the nearby township of Airland. If they could find a room there, they knew that it would be easier for them to keep in touch with Basadi; and before too long, they did find a suitable place. Meanwhile, Basadi remained in her own house, with the couple still occupying the outside rooms. By this time, their daughter had got married and her husband had joined the family there.

Many families in the townships shared this problem of overcrowding and living on top of each other. Sometimes families had to sacrifice all privacy and traditional ethics in order to have a roof over their heads.

Although they no longer lived with her, Basadi still regarded Khumo and Pelo as her children. In turn, they kept in regular contact with her. Khumo, in particular, was loving and dutiful towards his aunt-mother. Being the mature person she was, Basadi refused to interpret Pelo's rare visits to her as a rejection of their relationship. Instead, she made it a habit to call on them at least once a month on a Saturday afternoon. On these occasions, Pelo always received her with all due warmth and attention. This meant a great deal to Khumo.

Now aged about seventy, Basadi still enjoyed good health

and managed her household chores with remarkable ease and efficiency. Neighbours and relatives all commented on her agile movements and high standards of housekeeping. In her life at home, there were certain things which were a matter of routine. On her arrival back from work, she would have a cup of tea, open the windows and check that the house was tidy and in order. She would then sort out the clothes which she would wear to work the following day, wash and rinse the containers for her lunch and, after supper, pack her lunch and fill up her flask with tea. Finally, she would place these things in the bag she took to work. This had been her habit for many years.

On the surface, then, all seemed well with Basadi. But in recent months she had begun saying some very strange things to close friends, neighbours and relatives. She had been talking of her concern for her security and safety. To Khumo and his wife, she had even expressed a fear for her life – although she had mentioned no names in connection with her fear. Stranger still, she stated clearly that if she were to be reported dead, they should know that she would have died for the house. Khumo could make no sense of what she said; her utterings seemed far-fetched and unbounded, quite at odds with the self-confident and strong person that she was.

One day, Basadi withdrew a substantial amount from her savings book in order to pay her electricity bill at the rent office the following day. She also collected the documents relating to her house for the purpose, so it is said, of finalising the transfer of ownership of the house to Khumo. She told some neighbours that she was carrying out all these arrangements in the face of very frightening threats – that she had been told that if she dared to transfer the house to anybody in her family, she would be killed for it. But she made it clear that she intended to ignore these threats and to carry on with her plans. Once she got home from work, she carried out her normal routine of preparations for the next day; but this time she also placed the money and documents in her bag. And then, as usual, she retired to her bedroom.

The next morning – the morning on which she intended to carry out her plans – Basadi was reported dead. In shock, her family, relatives, friends and neighbours began to recall her warnings. But, of course, it was too late.

When the body was discovered, Khumo and his wife had already gone to work. They were contacted by phone and asked to come to their uncle's home to witness the tragedy that had shocked the neighbourhood. By the time they arrived there, neighbours had already reported the death to the police, who in turn had certified Basadi dead and had sent her corpse to the government mortuary. It was there, after a post-mortem, that the discovery was made that Basadi had not died from natural causes.

From that point, the law took its course. The couple who lived with Basadi were taken in for questioning, along with their daughter and son-in-law. They were soon released, and joined the family, friends and neighbours at Basadi's burial in the country. After their return from the funeral, the son-in-law was never seen in the neighbourhood again. The old couple moved away from the area; and their daughter rented a room alone.

Meanwhile, Khumo was granted legal rights to the house, as his aunt-mother had wished and planned.

Part Five

A Person is a Person Because of Another Person

One of the less desirable results of missionary education in South Africa was that older people have grown up with the belief that their traditional culture and values were 'primitive' and 'backward' when compared with western standards.

Over the years, living with the brutalities and hypocrisies of post-colonial and apartheid regimes, we have learned to look more critically at western claims of this kind. And we have also discovered anew the rich heritage of wisdom and compassion passed down to us by our parents, grandparents and great-grandparents.

It is something of a miracle that we have managed to retain any vestige of our traditional values. Our lives have been pushed and pulled in all directions according to the whim of governments which we have had no say in electing. The life of a black child in South Africa today is a series of endless problems, denials, challenges and confrontations. From the age of four or five, these boys and girls come face to face with problems which in any other society would be encountered by men of thirty or forty years of age. And how many grandmothers would say – as I have to say – that my own opportunities for education were far superior to those available to my childen and grandchildren in the black education system in South Africa?

Moral values are associated with an ordered, just way of life. It is no accident, then, that in the attempt to examine such values, the two stories here look back to the past – and on to the future – rather than focus on our fragmented present.

Lasting impressions

Neo grew up during the first fifteen years of this century as one of many young people in her maternal grandparents' home. This home was a family farm – Thaba Patchua in the province of the Orange Free State. Her grandparents had inherited the farm from their parents.

Every day, after the evening meal, Neo and the other young people would sit around the hearth to listen to popular traditional tales related by the elders. These were tales of fun, of mystery – and of untold imagination.

To this day, Neo retains very vivid memories of this period of her youth; and she continues to share these memories with young and old neighbours and friends. 'These were great years of joy and excitement,' she will tell you. 'We listened eagerly to our grandparents and other adults telling us many stories – tales of ghosts, of huge river snakes, of large birds said to have unsurpassed magical powers, and of Tikoloshe, a short, hairy being full of magical power.' And she concludes, 'Of course, we believed them to be true.'

Neo tells how the young people looked forward to summer evenings when they would sit outside on the *stoep* (verandah) of the house, excitedly looking out for some of these 'real' creatures which had captured their imagination. The children knew, of course, that these creatures would be visible only a long time after dusk since they shunned daylight. At these times, parents and all the other adults would be busy indoors, unaware of the drama that captured the minds of their young ones.

'As we sat outside,' Neo says, 'our minds and eyes directed towards the Leeu river which ran east of the homestead, one solitary light would emerge from nowhere, moving away from us at high speed and without sound. Suddenly, the light would turn back to where it came from, moving at the same speed and showing no sign of slowing up. Meanwhile, two or three similar lights would join the magnificent display.' According to Neo, the show carried on until a certain star, known as *Naledi ya Masa* (the Morning Star) vividly gave out its rays, signalling past midnight to those it entertained.

Neo will then tell you one of the stories that was most popular during the evening sessions round the hearth. This was the story about the huge snake known as the Ruler and Master of the Leeu River. With her eyes wide open as if to show the size of the snake, Neo will tell you: 'The enormous snake had one huge light on its head which lit up its surroundings as it steered out of the river after dusk in search of its prey and of the cow dung it liked to eat.' The children, of course, linked this one big eye of the river snake with the one bright light they used to see on the river. According to Neo's memory of the tale, this unusual snake-like creature moved along the banks of the river, determined to destroy any life it came across, be it human or animal, before it retreated again into the river.

As this story was told around the hearth, the listeners infected each other with fear and horror, letting out squeals of terror and alarm, and hiding behind each other. Meanwhile, the older listeners would murmur hush-hush noises like, 'Oh', 'Hmm', and 'Ssh'.

The next day, the happenings of the night before, both real and imaginary, were topics of great interest for all the youngsters. Each of the children would develop their own versions of what they had seen or heard. And in this way they confirmed what they believed they saw and experienced.

The usual thing was to interpret these snakes, queer birds and strange creatures as the spirits of dead people who had failed to find rest after death. The Ruler and Master of the River, in particular, was always said to have the power to draw anyone, young or old, into its clutches.

And so all the youngsters emerged from these experiences with powerful images of the bright and dark sides of the world around them. These images would accompany them, as they accompanied Neo, all through their later life.

When Neo went to school and met young people from urban communities, she found herself listening to stories from films and bioscopes. She would have very much liked to share with her new friends some of her early experiences in the countryside. But she was inhibited about doing this as she felt that she would make herself a laughing stock with her stories of ghosts and river snakes.

Neo became a teacher and then qualified as a social worker, practising in urban areas. Over the years, as she got to know her colleagues well, there were many discussions of their different childhood and adolescent experiences. To her pleasure and surprise, Neo found that many of her colleagues had had similar experiences to her own. This discovery helped her to reflect on her past and begin to appreciate the wealth it had given her. Her self-confidence grew and she began to lose her inhibitions about her traditional upbringing.

Neo then found that folklore and traditional entertainment could be put to very effective use in the practice of social work. More and more, she came to realise the importance of the values, standards and practices of her own people. Soon she was able to share with pride and confidence her deep knowledge of the folklore, music, dances, costumes, dishes and home medicines traditional to the community.

Many of her colleagues began to seek her advice and guidance when they were organising rehearsals for youth festivals and competitions. Neo found it very reassuring to know that she had so much to contribute to the growth and development of her community. It gave her considerable satisfaction, too, to be asked for advice and guidance by colleagues from other racial groups, particularly whites: so often in the past such colleagues had given the strong impression that they knew all there was to know about black people – their culture, customs and overall way of life.

Her new role brought Neo professional recognition and a fresh image at work. So it was not surprising that her name was at the top of the list when her agency chose a delegate for a programme to be run in the UK and later in the USA.

During that time overseas, she was exposed to the international scene at many levels. She gained direct experience of the customs of the people of different countries; and, in return, she shared with other delegates the dances, music, folklore and customs of her people back home. This mutual sharing gave Neo the opportunity to compare her own culture with those of other countries.

As part of the programme, Neo was assigned to some intensive small group work with two delegates from different countries. Since the work – exciting but challenging – was based in the cities of Columbus and Dayton, the three colleagues lived in a Residence Center in Dayton. Living close together in this way enabled them to plan their work together and also to share their leisure time.

The Center was a tall building with four floors. Neo was given a room of her own, while her two colleagues shared a room in another wing of the building. At the beginning, Neo felt rather lonely and isolated; but she soon adjusted to being on her own and indeed rather enjoyed being able to concentrate fully on her work and on her correspondence. Occasionally, she would join her colleagues for a relaxed chat; and all three got into the habit of having meals and going for walks together.

During Neo's second weekend in Dayton, a group of young women from the city and its suburbs assembled at the Residence Center for a seminar. Normally quiet and calm, the Center was transformed by the arrival of the young people. The surroundings rippled with laughter and excited conversation, interrupted from time to time by the shouts of friends who had not seen one another for a long time. When the noise reached quite extraordinary levels, the three international delegates went downstairs to see what was going on. As they stood watching the girls moving from the changing rooms towards the swimming pool, they agreed that the Center had really come alive that day and that the joyful spirits of the young people had broken that monotony which had previously marked the Center.

This was the first time since her arrival in the country that Neo had seen so many young black women together. As she looked at them, she was embarrassed to notice that a number of the girls looked pregnant. She thought immediately about the young girls at home in South Africa who found themselves in a similar situation. She had heard much more about the progressive and democratic nature of great countries like America; and she found it difficult to reconcile what she saw with what she had heard about the country. She noticed that many of the girls who were pregnant also seemed very calm and happy. Neo wondered whether this meant that to be in this condition at that age was accepted as quite normal in American society. Eventually, Neo came to the conclusion that the plight of blacks was almost the same the world over. She felt pain and hurt inside. Not in this country too, she thought, time and again. She longed to reach out to these girls; and, eventually, she did manage to have a conversation with several of them.

As she chatted with her colleagues later, Neo's mind was filled with many unanswered questions. And even when she got back to her room, her mind was still clouded with uneasy thoughts. But she took her bath, sorted out her work for the next day, locked the door, turned out the light and, before too long, fell into a deep sleep.

That night, Neo was roused from sleep by what she

thought was a very bad dream. If indeed it was a dream, it was one that took her right back to her childhood days. She woke up with a heavy thump in her heart. This is how she describes what happened:

'From a deep sleep, I was aroused by the noise of a screeching, stopping lift and the shutting of its door. It was as if the door had been pushed by a heavy, strong force. Then came sharp footsteps as if someone had come walking out of the lift. The sound of the heels of her shoes rang sharply in my ears. By that time, I knew that I was awake and in my full senses. The footsteps came straight towards my room. I listened, panting for breath and shivering helplessly under the sheets; there was no one there that I could shake and ask, "Do you hear what I hear?" The ting! ting! ting! sharp steps stopped dead at my door. I was sweating and breathing heavily. I raised my head and opened my eyes. Bright light was flooding my room from the bottom of the door. I thought that someone was turning the doorknob. Thank God the door was locked. At that point, I froze with fright.'

Neo goes on: 'As if very angry, the steps moved back from where they had come, rapping down as if they would crack the floor. Then followed the harsh opening and shutting of the lift door, with the lift going down at a terrific speed. I gave a great sigh of relief, believing that the lady's steps were gone for ever. I would have given anything to find out what time it was; but I was so frightened that I didn't dare to move and look at my watch. This was not the end, though. In a very short time, the whole performance was repeated in the same sequence. Two, three, four times, it all happened again, with only five or ten minutes in between.'

During this time of terror, Neo prayed for protection from harm. She wished that her trip was ending that day. She longed to be back home with her family and friends. She lost all interest in travelling and coming across new people and experiences – at least for the duration of that nightmare. She promised her Creator to serve Him without fail if she was spared from this ordeal. She prayed for sunrise. She told herself she would never sleep alone in that room again.

Neo thinks that she must have passed out for a time. She woke to a room full of sunshine, but with a very clear memory of what had happened the night before. Still trembling with fear, she got out of bed but found that, despite the bright light, she was still scared to open the door. Finally, she forced herself to do so and made straight for her colleagues' bedroom. She shared her frightening ordeal with them and asked if they had heard anything. They listened to her with disbelief, but so convincing was her description that they did not challenge what she said. Hardly waiting for a response from them, Neo asked them whether they thought she should report her experience to the lady in charge of the Residence. They hesitated, but did not say that she should not do so. Deep down, Neo had already decided that she would tell everything to the head of the Residence Center.

Neo went back to tidy her room before going in search of her. As she was clearing up her things, she was startled by a knock on the door. On her 'Come in', one of the women cleaners entered. They exchanged greetings; then, reluctantly, Neo shared with her her recent terrifying experience. She expected no particular response other than perhaps some sympathy. Instead, the woman looked at Neo with a face full of awe, then tried to hide her reaction. Taking all this in, Neo became suspicious and asked, 'Is there anything unusual about this building?' As if afraid there was someone within hearing distance, the woman looked around her and, almost whispering, replied in a strange, deep voice, 'Lady, there is only one piece of advice I can give you about this place. Please never put out your light when you go to bed. Keep it on through the night.'

The woman's words and manner were so odd that Neo almost burst out laughing. But she was also startled. 'Why?' she asked the woman. 'Is this room spooky?' She remembered the many ghost stories she had listened to during her childhood days back home. The woman replied, 'I know nothing about spooks or ghosts – from what I have heard, this whole residence is new. But I have been told that the old building which stood here many, many years ago was washed away by heavy storms and floods, and that many people died in that tragedy.' Neo stood there dumbfounded as she drew her own conclusions from the woman's words.

This information cleared away Neo's few, lingering doubts about whether or not to give a report of her experiences to the head of the Residence Center. Without checking again with her colleagues, she went straight to the office of the General Secretary. There she reported all that had transpired the night before. The intensity of the fear she had experienced expelled all her worries about being labelled superstitious and, as she told her story, she was almost unmindful of the impression she made on the Secretary. Her strongest concern was to avoid having to go through another night like the previous one.

To Neo's surprise, the lady in charge of the institution did not subject her to a barrage of questions. She simply turned to her and said, 'I am sorry to hear of this unsettling experience of yours. I will do all I can to find you accommodation, even if it is with private individuals. Would you mind that?' Without hesitation, Neo responded, 'I will go anywhere as long as I do not have to stay in that room.' Immediately, with Neo still sitting in the office, the head of the Center picked up her telephone and spoke to someone, finding quite neutral words to explain why Neo wished to leave. She was obviously determined to find alternative accommodation for Neo. The person she was speaking to did not ask many questions either and almost at once agreed to put Neo up. Silently, Neo concluded that her problem must be familiar to the management there.

That evening, Neo moved in with her new hosts – a local priest and his wife. She joined her colleagues every morning after breakfast. To begin with, she missed the company of her colleagues in the early part of the morning, but she soon adjusted to her new routine.

By this time, many aspects of her visit to America were setting Neo's mind to work. Her most recent experience brought home to her the fact that the kind of stories which she had heard in her community since childhood were not peculiar to her people. The cleaning woman, Neo had not been slow to notice, had somehow managed to refer to ghosts without acknowledging that she herself was in any way what might be called 'superstitious'. And yet, Neo reflected with disgust, foreigners were only too ready to say out loud that the black people of South Africa were different from westerners in that they were both ignorant and superstitious.

Turning such thoughts round in her mind, Neo began to take a much more critical look at the assumptions which, over the years, she had been led to make about European standards and ways of living. What was the truth behind the words – the words which emphasised civilised ways and manners, a high rate of literacy, emancipation from ignorance and superstition, and high moral standards? Some of the words were true, she knew that. But others – well, Neo only had to remember her conversations with the pregnant young women to identify some very serious shortcomings in these so-called 'civilised' communities.

Neo had been horrified to hear a girl of about thirteen years of age talk freely about being compelled to sleep with men to earn a living because her family was too poor to meet its basic needs. Neo found it appalling that any girl should be forced to use her body in this way in order to earn the money needed to keep attending school. The only conclusion she could reach was that all, or most, western countries treated black people like third-class human beings. In Neo's mind, any person or government that discriminated on a colour or a race basis was far from being civilised.

The philosophy of her own people back home rang loud

and clear in her ears. Six different languages told the same story:

'*Muthu ndi muthu nga munwe*'   (Sevenda)
'*Motho ke motho ka motho yo mangwe*'   (Setswana)
'*Umtu ngo mtu ngabanye*'   (Xosa)
'*Motho ke motho ka motho e mong*'   (Southern Sotho)
'*Umtu ngo mtu ngo monye umtu*'   (Zulu)
'*Umuntfu ngumuntfu ngalo munye muntfu*'   (Swasi)

The literal meaning of the saying is: 'A person is a person because of another person'. This philosophy, Neo knew, lays a foundation for interchange and interaction with other people, whether as individuals or as groups. It sets standards for the way people live together. The implications of the saying go far beyond the English expression, 'No man is an island'. The saying of Neo's people provides a basis for communal living; it implies a constant state of mutual interdependence.

Neo recalled how, as a little girl, she witnessed poor whites visit her grandparents' home. There they were received with warm hospitality and kindness, being invited to join the family in wholesome meals. She remembered clearly that, in her community at the turn of the century, the colour of a person's skin did not diminish their worth as a human being.

With all these thoughts crossing her mind, Neo came to the conclusion: 'Despite the denial of opportunities to my people back home – the political, economic, educational, social and cultural opportunities offered to, and enjoyed in abundance by, other race groups in that country – I stand up and declare with no fear of contradiction that it takes a great people to survive what we have survived. It is for this reason that I say to anyone who will listen, "Don't judge them by what they don't have – but rather by the values which they express in their culture." With us, one man's success blossoms out of another man's support. We are a people who prize human values far above materialistic gain. And this philosophy of ours has survived harsh decades of conquest and oppression. There is something truly to wonder at.'

Life for the black youngsters of that era

At the turn of the century, many black families depended on the land for their living and livelihood. Some owned large areas of land; others owned permanent homes on small individual patches or on communal land. In normal times, the land rewarded the people's efforts by providing food and more. In times of drought or other disasters, people could live on the surplus that they had stored.

That land was the pride and joy of those who owned it and of the community as a whole. They looked on it as home and as their hope for the future. Labour on such land was joyfully undertaken: the labourers knew that through caring for the land, they were also looking to the future of their children and their children's children.

Those on communal ground devised a formula for the division of land for crop cultivation. A separate piece of land was set apart for grazing. To ensure good grazing, the residents of communal land kept strict control over the movements of their animals. Communal land was maintained by the labour of the resident on the land.

On private land, things were different. Here, the work was done by temporary labourers unconnected with the farm, or by contractors who had their permanent homes on the farm.

Temporary labourers were sometimes single men and women and sometimes whole families. These labourers herded livestock, ploughed the land, looked after the crops, and transported grain by ox wagon – a time-consuming business. The labourers often lived not far from the home farm and thus were on constant call for the odd jobs that always seemed to need doing. If they worked well, these labourers would quite often attain a more permanent status.

The other labourers – the contractors – were drawn from those who had a permanent home of their own on the farm and who had been allocated land to cultivate for their seasonal crops along with some rights to keep livestock. Some members of this group were self-sufficient, able to make a living out of the land allocated to them. Others needed to do extra work to augment their income. It was in this latter group that the landowner found the handymen he needed for jobs involving plumbing, carpentry and painting. Some of these permanent residents established and maintained splendid vegetable gardens; others were known to be exceptionally good at milking cows.

Many of the young people on the farm came from such families. When a school was provided for the farm population, this would serve as a central meeting place for young people from all walks of life. There they would work and play together, regardless of their status or background. While growing up together – making friendships, breaking friendships, quarrelling and making up – some of these young people formed groups for singing and dancing, thus greatly developing their natural abilities. Some of these groups made up the star attraction in school and Sunday school concerts and other public events.

In the 1920s, it was common for these 'farm schools' to be built, with the help of the permanent residents on the farm, on land owned by black farmers. All members of these communities were keen that the younger generation should have an opportunity to learn to read and write. The younger children would attend school full-time; the older ones, who were already in regular employment, would attend night-school classes run by the same teachers.

The children in these communities led busy and productive lives. They had many household duties allocated to them in addition to their school work. Each child would be assigned particular tasks such as sweeping and cleaning certain rooms, fetching water from the fountain, or collecting and washing dishes after meals. Sometimes, too, the children would be expected to go out to collect fuel for the fire – wood, mealie cobs or cow dung.

During harvest time, the young people looked forward to running errands for their elders. They were always ready, for example, to transport water to a work camp. The young-sters took a real pride in carrying out such duties well.

The children of these communities also found plenty of time in which to play. *Mantlwantlwane* ('housie-housie') was a favourite game of theirs. They would build mud houses of the right size for their dolls and then they would furnish these houses with equipment made out of empty match-boxes, broken china, and so on. All necessary furniture – cupboards, tables, chairs – was provided for the owners of the houses, who were ragdolls, dressed up and played with as human characters. These dolls spoke, laughed and cried through the voices of those who made them. They paid one another social visits. And sometimes they went to offer comfort and support when the doll community had been afflicted by illness or death. . .

In one home on a farm, all those years ago, a group of children brought their play close to an event in their real lives. These children loved the family pets – when it suited them. One day, they noticed a sickly cat near the homestead. On several occasions they tried offering it milk, but the cat would not drink. The adults in the family barely listened to the children's reports of the situation. Nothing daunted, the children followed the sick cat to its dying day. And then, instead of reporting the death to the family, they organised a decent funeral for the animal. The chief mourners were ragdolls who sobbed and wept through the voices of their makers, two young girls. The roles of gravedigger and pall-bearer were taken by the two boys of the group. And so the children rehearsed for their parts in later life. The youngsters missed the cat long after its burial.

Saturdays were spent by these children in roaming the countryside, exploring the surroundings of the farm. They would walk to the fields on either side of the river running through the farm. There they would pick wild fruits (*monak-aladi*) and wild flowers, and experiment to see which plants yielded the best sap to use in sticking paper together or in re-assembling broken bits of china for the 'housie-housie' game. There were many lizards in the fields, but since they were frightened of these creatures, the children would observe them and compare them – but stay very clear of them. Snakes, too, filled the children with fear; but, again, they liked to watch them from a distance.

Some days, disobeying strict instructions from their elders, they would sit under willow trees in an area alleged to have very poisonous snakes. Here the youngsters would listen to the birds jumping from twig to twig, singing and making beautiful calls. In turn, the children would imitate the sounds made by the birds. Later, they would listen to each other and then match the sounds with the kind of bird that would make them. This was always an engaging and inspiring activity for them.

Two girls in that group developed a great love for horses, to the point that they picked out as their own two of their family's animals. They then took great pleasure in riding round the farm. When they were a little older, they used to ride to the local store to fetch the family's post which would have been brought there from the nearest railway station by the shopkeeper. Every day, it was a great treat for the two girls to make this excursion on horseback.

At school, the youngsters started a habit of sharing and

swapping lunch dishes. The poorer children – particularly those who came from farms owned by whites – used to bring a liquid, mealie-meal porridge known as *seqhaqhabola*, a very tasty dish if well prepared. The children from more well-to-do homes brought sandwiches of butter and jam. Those who brought the porridge would swap with those who brought sandwiches. It was a moment keenly anticipated by those who joined in the swapping. Some children – those who had strict parents – were unable to join in and so missed a great deal of excitement.

To this day, when some of these old school mates meet, they remember with laughter and joy this early trading of theirs. The quantity of food swapped was not the main issue. The important thing was the 'product' swapped. Of course, in those years and in that setting, the porridge, bread, butter and jam were all homemade.

In black communities, both rural and urban, music has always been the focus for many events. And, for these young people, song and dance were foremost in their minds when it came to entertainment and recreation. Some songs were used for specific games. In one, for example, young people sitting in a circle would each put a small round stone in front of them. When they started to sing, '*Ke thubile koniki* (I have broken the cup)', each member of the circle would move her stone anti-clockwise. If a player was slow and stones piled up in front of her, she would have to leave the game. Another 'sitting' game was *Aumana Maskenki* (Granny Maskenki). Here, the team would just sit in a row and sing, swaying from side to side.

And then there were the skipping songs. '*Kgosi ya Mawatle*' ('The King of the Seas') was sung to keep the rhythm in skipping, the song changing tempo after a team of skippers had done one round. The winners were those who kept the pace up to the quickest tempo. There were many other songs used in games, and all were creative and enjoyable.

Traditional song and dance was very popular with all age

groups in this particular community. Many of the labourers came from Lesotho, so the music, dance and folklore which formed the centre of the entertainment came largely from the Sesotho culture. The appropriate time for such entertainment was in the evenings, when there was a full moon. On such evenings, the children would complete their household duties in record time in order to join in the festivities from the start.

During the evening, there would always be a great variety of songs and dances. Early on, the best performers would be spotted, and soloists of great ability would often lead the singing. Nearly everyone would join in the singing and dancing. It was generally only older people – or very shy young ones – who simply watched the proceedings. These occasions were marked by a great sense of order and responsibility. When the performance ended, participants and spectators all walked in groups to their homes.

Story-telling (*Ditshomo*) sessions were also great favourites. These would take place round an open-air fire after the evening meal. Some people think that the stories were told only by elderly people; but this is not how it was. It is true that the old people were wonderful story-tellers – but the young people listened and learned, cultivated the art and ended up, many of them, as great story-tellers themselves.

And then there were what might be called 'party games'. In one of these, known as '*Senyamo*', the leader would start by saying the word '*Senyamo*' ('Choose') to a particular person. This person would then respond by saying '*Se mang?*' ('Who?'). The leader would then announce the name of the person he wanted chosen. If the respondent liked the person, she would reply, '*Ka shoa*', meaning 'I die' – it being understood, of course, that she meant that she was dying of love for that person. . . If she rejected the person, she would say, '*Hlotse*' ('I don't love him'). The fun of this game lay in what happened when the name of someone's girlfriend or boyfriend was announced: the respondent would blush and giggle amid the laughter and yells of the other young people. Sometimes, too, the leader would give out the name of an ugly, uninteresting person; that also created an atmosphere of fun and laughter.

'*Malatadiana Tsela*' was a game which tested the powers of memory and observation. Twelve grains of mealie were placed in a row, the last nine being piled one on top of the other. Two people would take part in this game, one of them blindfolded. While the 'blind' player sang, he or she had to pick up each grain, trying to remember the sequence of the grains – whether packed singly or two together. The player would have to keep repeating the game until all the grains on top were removed. The other player checks what the blindfolded player does.

Working, studying, singing, dancing and playing games – that was how the people lived in those days. And all the time the country life enriched the young people with its healthy fresh air and beautiful scenery. This all laid a firm foundation for formal education and personal growth. How different it was from life in the so-called 'homelands' of today – raped as they are of beauty, vitality and cultural heritage.